THE CLASS REUNION

A PSYCHOLOGICAL SUSPENSE THRILLER

N. L. HINKENS

Text copyright @ 2020 Norma Hinkens

Published by Dunecadia Publishing, California

ISBN: 978-1-947890-25-1

Cover by: **www.derangeddoctordesign.com**

Editing by: **www.jeanette-morris.com/first-impressions-writing**

1

Heather Nelson never slept the night before the anniversary of what she'd done. She had concluded years ago that it was far better to work a night shift than wrestle with the haunting memories through the long, lonely hours until the sun came up again.

Sinking down into the seat of her unobtrusive Buick, she reached for her stainless-steel coffee mug, resigned to an extended evening of surveillance. The wealthy client who had hired her for this particular job suspected her infamous producer husband was cheating on her with his leggy, nineteen-year-old assistant. Gut instincts were usually right, but they didn't hold up in divorce court.

That's where Heather and her trusty telephoto lens came in, furtively cataloguing the necessary incriminating evidence to swing a custody case or invoke a prenup stripping an adulterous party of any share of the marital assets. Heather had considered branching out from the whole sleazy cheating spouse underworld and moving into a more intriguing field, but the money was simply too good to let it go. Like it or not, she excelled at making a living on the failed relationships of others. Her reputation as a tenacious private investigator had grown steadily over the years, and many of LA's wealthiest celebrities had become her clients —a lucrative customer base that guaranteed a steady income stream, and even repeat customers.

Falling into this line of work had been a lucky break of sorts. Growing up on a farm in Iowa, she couldn't wait to leave the monotonous pace of rural life behind. But after what happened to her younger sister, Violet, Heather had abandoned her plans for college. She had felt obligated to stick around and protect her sister—the way she should have done that awful night when both their lives had changed forever.

She ended up taking a job bartending in nearby Davenport and struck up a friendship with one of her regular patrons, a grouchy man in his sixties with a long, gray ponytail who turned out to be a veteran PI with an arsenal of stories. They got into some interesting conversations about cases he'd worked on, and, before long, he convinced her she had a knack for the trade and offered her a job. She had hung up her bar towels and washed out her jiggers and blender for the last time that night. From the outset, it felt like a good fit, a way to right societal wrongs—something she was passionate about.

Heather blew out a heavy breath and adjusted her position in the seat, her gaze planted on the shadowy building opposite, watching for any sign of the cheating spouse in question. It was his twin three-year-old daughters she felt sorry for. They were too young to understand that their parents would be spending the best part of the next few years wrestling in court over assets—using them as pawns in every play that was made. A nauseating prospect that only cemented her commitment to singleness. At thirty-eight, she had never come close to being engaged, let alone married. But if Heather was being honest with herself, the dysfunction she had witnessed over the years at her job wasn't the real reason she was unwilling to commit to a relationship. It was because of what had happened to Violet in high school. And what Heather had done about it afterward.

Her phone buzzed and she glanced at the unknown number on the screen. Possibly a new client. She straightened up in her seat and cleared her throat, preparing to slip into the professional spiel that rolled effortlessly from her tongue after two decades in the trade. "Heather Nelson speaking."

After a lengthy pause, a man's voice asked, "Is this Integrity Investigations?"

"It is."

"I ... wasn't sure—" the man stammered.

"Discretion is key," Heather hastened to explain. "Surveillance targets sometimes find my number in a client's phone and call to see who answers. The last thing I want to do is tip them off to the fact that they're being investigated."

"Ah, of course. That makes perfect sense." The man hesitated as if prompting Heather to take the reins.

"How can I help?" she went on, curbing her impatience at the faltering conversation. It was a mistake to press new clients. Trust was a process.

"I need the services of a private investigator—my associate recommended you. I have reason to believe my wife is cheating on me. Well, it's only a suspicion really. You see ..."

Heather let him ramble on, her gaze still fixed on the high-rent apartment building on the other side of the street. She knew better than to interrupt. Her reputation was partly built on her PI skills, but equal parts on tact and discretion.

Infidelity cases were notoriously sensitive. No matter how mentally prepared a client was for the news, the emotional shock still sometimes hit like a bomb blast. She had seen grown men crumble and cry after providing them with proof of what they already suspected. Once, she'd witnessed a tiny slip of a woman reduce a three-hundred-thousand-dollar sports car to scrap metal with a hammer.

As soon as the man hung up, she Googled his name and discovered that Karan Patel was an introverted tech company CEO who rarely gave interviews. His much younger wife was an ex-model turned socialite—which Heather understood as a blanket term in LA for anyone whose life revolved around buffing, styling, primping, and networking their way on to exclusive party lists. She scrolled through some Google images. The perfectly coiffed Mrs. Patel seemed to prefer being photographed on the arms of celebrity actors than at her nondescript bespectacled husband's side. Karan was likely right about her roving ways. His years of computer coding in the background was now bankrolling her time in the limelight. Heather had never embraced the LA lifestyle, preferring her homegrown Iowan roots, where you didn't know who had money and who didn't, and no one cared either way. Truth be told, she missed the wide-open spaces, the days when a traffic jam consisted of being stuck behind a tractor or a cattle trailer.

A movement in the doorway of the building she was surveilling caught her attention. She tossed her phone on the passenger seat and reached for her camera. She'd invested in the best equipment available, and it had paid for itself many times over. She could outgun the paparazzi when it came to surveillance, and she was fairly certain she could go toe-to-toe with the CIA in a pinch.

A tall, bearded man with an expensive suit jacket slung

carelessly over one shoulder emerged from the doorway, his other arm around the waist of the blonde woman at his side. He threw back his head and laughed at something she said as the two made their way to the adjacent parking lot. Heather expertly snapped a series of photos in quick succession before losing sight of the pair. She waited until their car emerged from the parking lot and then followed at a discreet distance until they pulled up outside a small but exclusive Italian restaurant.

The two-timing producer tossed his keys to the parking valet before ushering the woman up the steps. Heather snapped several more shots as the two entered the restaurant. Once they were out of sight, she laid her camera on the seat next to her. She had more than enough evidence to confirm her client's suspicions, but a photo of the pair locking lips would be a bonus. She debated hanging out for an hour or two and waiting for the couple to leave. With a few drinks in them, they were likely to be a lot more amorous.

Her phone beeped with an incoming email and she reached for it as she adjusted the baseball cap on her head. She frowned at the sender's name. *Reagan Evans*. She hadn't seen Reagan since she'd moved to LA—she'd been Reagan Butler back then. Heather had gotten an invitation to her wedding last year but declined it, just like she'd turned down all the other invitations necessitating a return trip to Iowa.

Curious, she opened the email.

Hey Heather,

I got your contact info from your website. I know you haven't been in touch with the group for a while, so I wasn't sure if you had heard about Lindsay. Such a horrific thing to happen! Here's a link to the local news article so you can read it for yourself. I'm so sorry, I know you guys were close. By the way, I'm sure you got the invitation to the reunion. We'd love to see you again—especially now, after what happened to Lindsay. We're including a special tribute to her in the program. Please think about it. My number is (563) 271-3349.

Regards,
Reagan

A DULL THUD like a distant explosion sounded deep inside Heather's chest. Lindsay Robinson was the only member of their once tight-knit student council group that she had kept up with in the twelve years she'd been living in LA, and even that had deteriorated into a quick call at Christmas, or a perfunctory email exchange—an obligation tied to a dark secret. Lindsay was the one person Heather had told what she'd done that awful night and, thankfully, Lindsay had kept her mouth shut. Not even Violet knew the truth, and Heather had no intention of telling her. For better or for worse, what was done, was done.

2

W ith a growing sense of apprehension, Heather clicked the link in Reagan's email and stared impatiently at the screen until the *Quad City Herald's* website loaded. As she scanned the headline, the breath seeped from her lungs.

Davenport Woman Dies From Rattlesnake Bite.

A biker on an evening ride on a remote, muddy section of the Great River Trail suffered a fatal rattlesnake bite after her bike spun out and she was thrown into the brush. Police believe she was knocked unconscious when she hit her head on a rock near to where a snake was nesting. Tragically, the woman's body was not discovered until the following morning when a jogger spotted her abandoned bicycle lying at the side of the trail.

Fist pressed to her mouth, Heather reread the article several times until the words were engraved on her mind. It was too shocking to comprehend. A freak accident with an unimaginably grisly ending. How could Lindsay be gone just like that? Of all of them, she should have lived the longest—she'd always been such a health nut with her matcha green tea smoothies and fermented salads. Not to mention the fact that she was an incredible athlete, competing across the country in professional bike races. She had taken a few spills before, but never suffered anything more than cuts and bruises. It didn't make sense. Lindsay was an expert at navigating technical trails. It was hard to imagine how a little mud could have thrown her off her bike.

Heather felt sick to her stomach picturing Lindsay's last moments. The thought of her lying in the brush, unconscious and helpless, while a rattlesnake slithered over her was particularly horrifying. Her thoughts spiraled quickly downward. Had Lindsay suffered as the venom took hold? Or perhaps, mercifully, she'd been oblivious to what was happening. Heather couldn't imagine anything worse than dying alone as the cold and darkness moved in to take you. She rubbed her shaking hands on her thighs. In all likelihood, Lindsay hadn't regained consciousness. She would have called 911 if she'd been able. And if she couldn't get a signal, she would have crawled out of there if she'd had to. That was the type of person she was.

Yanking off her baseball cap, Heather tossed it on the passenger seat. She had lost all interest in hanging around outside the restaurant until her client's errant spouse and his blonde date reemerged. All she wanted to do was get home and absorb the shock ricocheting through her body. Her head pounded as she put the car in gear. The article Reagan had sent her was dated a week ago which meant the funeral had most likely already taken place. She should have been there, for Lindsay's mother's sake. Pam must be devastated at the loss of her only child. Heather peeled out of her parking spot and accelerated down the street, her pulse thundering in her ears. She hadn't set foot in Iowa since leaving for LA twelve years earlier. Some part of her had hoped that by staying away, her secret would fade into a nothingness—almost as if it had all been a bad dream. The thought of going back to where it had happened sent her into a cold sweat.

Her breath came in short, sharp stabs as the memory of that night resurfaced with a vengeance—the pleading look in his eyes, his fingers smearing blood across the glass in a last-ditch cry for help. All these years later, and it still felt like yesterday. She shuddered and took a hasty swig of coffee from her travel mug, her throat as dry as sandpaper. She dreaded to think what would have happened if anyone had found out what she'd done. But that was no longer a concern. Her secret was now rotting in the grave along with Lindsay.

Wiping a trembling hand over her brow, Heather pulled into the underground parking structure of the luxury condominium complex where she lived. She switched off the engine and reached for her camera bag. Maybe she should reconsider and go back for her twentieth class reunion after all. In light of what had happened, it seemed like the appropriate thing to do—Lindsay had wanted her to go. If nothing else, Reagan and the others would appreciate the gesture. And that way she could express her condolences to Lindsay's mother in person. The reunion was still six weeks away. That gave her plenty of time between now and then to wrap up her current cases, including the sleazy producer and the reclusive Karan Patel.

Inside her condominium, Heather's five-year-old Shih tzu, Phoebe, raced to greet her, then tore around the white-tiled floor chasing her tail in circles until Heather fetched her a treat. "Sit pretty," she said, waiting until Phoebe sat back on her haunches and held up her front paws. "Good girl!" Heather cooed, tossing her a miniature doggie biscuit.

She walked over to her refrigerator and surveyed the bleak array of options for dinner. In her panic to get home, she'd forgotten to pick up anything. Mostly, she lived on takeout or whatever the deli at the corner market had left over that didn't look like it had been sitting under a heat lamp for half its allotted lifespan.

After pulling out a carton of leftover chow mein, Heather plonked herself down at the kitchen table to eat. As she chewed on her food, her mind drifted back to the home in Iowa where she'd grown up. She and Violet had enjoyed a relatively happy childhood—idyllic some might call it. Two loving, if overly strict, parents, doting grandparents, a farm full of animals and adventure, and enough money for a yearly road trip to one of the national parks. What had happened to Violet had changed everything. It was almost as if life had a strange filter on it from that point on that sucked the color from things, casting unsavory shadows on everyone she met, disintegrating her trust in people.

Heather deeply regretted lying to her parents that night. Violet had begged her not to tell them what happened—insisting she couldn't bear the thought of everyone at school finding out and talking about her behind her back. Years later, when she was getting married, she broke down and told them the truth. Naturally, they were devastated, and wracked with guilt to think their daughter had gone for years without any justice. Six months later, their father suffered a fatal heart attack, and their mother developed early onset Alzheimer's and died at only fifty-nine years of age. Heather hadn't been able to stop any of their lives unraveling.

Stomach roiling, she shoved the carton of food aside and pulled out her phone. After reading through Reagan's email again, she set her lips in a resolute line and dialed the number.

"Hello?" a sleepy voice said.

Her heart jolted at the sound of Reagan's voice—a distant echo from the past.

"Hi, Reagan. It's Heather—Heather Nelson."

There was a sharp intake of breath on the other end of the line and then Reagan said, "Just a minute while I go downstairs. Dave's asleep."

Heather groaned inwardly. She'd forgotten to check the time before she called. It was already 11:15 p.m. in Iowa.

"Are you still there?" Reagan asked.

"Yes. Listen, I'm sorry to call this late. I completely spaced out on the time. I just got off work and saw your email."

"Don't worry about it," Reagan responded, sounding as if she was stifling a yawn. "It's good to hear from you. We're all in shock. It was such a horrific thing to happen—and to Lindsay of all people. I can't bear to think about it."

Heather bit her lip, unexpected tears pricking her eyes. "Did I miss the funeral?"

"Her mother didn't want one. She was cremated." Reagan hesitated. "There's no easy way to tell you this, but her injuries were pretty horrific. They didn't mention it in the news article, but she was bitten twice--once in the face. One of the officers at the scene is a cousin of Dave's. He said she was so swollen she was almost unrecognizable."

Heather scrunched her eyes shut, the phone clamped to her ear. Chow mein churned in her belly. "Poor Pam," she rasped.

"She's gutted. I'm surprised she hasn't contacted you," Reagan said.

"To be honest, Lindsay and I haven't been in touch much

lately—Christmas, birthdays, the odd email, that's about it. We've both been so busy."

There was another long pause, and then Reagan said, "Look, I know you've got this highfalutin PI firm in LA now, but it would be good to see you again, for old time's sake. The reunion's only six weeks away. Like I mentioned, the former student council members are going to do something special to honor Lindsay that night. I know we've had our differences in the past, but it would be great if you could be there too."

Heather blew out a breath. "I can probably pull it off if I move some things around."

"Wonderful!" Reagan gushed. "I'll reserve a seat at our table for you."

Heather hung up and buried her face in her hands. A lone tear slid down her cheek. Lindsay had kept her secret safe all these years—it was up to her now to protect Lindsay's.

3

Heather spotted Reagan first as she walked out into the arrival terminal pulling her black roller case behind her. Her backpack and most of her clothes were black too, with the odd gray or other coordinating neutral thrown in to refute any notion that she worked at a funeral home. It wasn't that she disliked color. Black was merely a practical choice that made her job of blending into a crowd that much easier when she was shadowing a target. As she spent the bulk of her time working, or perfecting her skills at the gun range, a more vibrant wardrobe would serve no purpose other than to highlight her non-existent social life.

Despite not having seen her former classmate in over a decade, Heather recognized Reagan immediately—the dark, wavy hair cascading around her pale, narrow face, the preoccupied slant of her shoulders, the impatient stance, one knee bent, tapping her toes. Reagan was oblivious to her arrival, typing furiously into her phone, a deep cleft in evidence between her brows. She had always been the uptight sort with a burning need to control, expecting everyone in her circle to kowtow to her. And they generally did. She had desperately wanted the position of class president their senior year, but she'd been trailing behind Heather in votes—at least until rumors started circulating that Heather was HIV positive. She'd always had a sneaking suspicion that Reagan was behind the rumors, but she had no way to prove it.

Heather felt a small pang of anxiety in the pit of her stomach as she strode toward her. She wasn't sure how Reagan was going to react to seeing her again. She would have preferred to stay with Violet and her husband, Boyd, but they were in New York on business. Reagan's invitation to stay with her and her new husband, Dave, had sounded sincere on the phone, but they'd both been in shock at Lindsay's unexpected death, feeling the need to reconnect over the tragedy. Would they have anything to talk about beyond that? Heather hadn't even made the effort to attend Reagan's wedding last year. And, despite having worked together on the student council, the underlying tension between them their senior year had eroded their friendship.

In the end, Reagan's campaign had been successful— partly due to the other student council members endorsing her. They had tried to soften the blow by assuring Heather that it was nothing personal. It was simply a fact that with all the rumors going around about her, Reagan was more likely to secure the vote. None of them knew what had happened to Violet a few weeks earlier, or the heartache Heather was hiding over it. They only knew she'd begun to distance herself from them around the time the rumors started.

Heather sucked in a breath, steeling herself for the impending awkward reunion. Now that she was here, she was second-guessing her decision to come. A trip down memory lane was a terrifying proposition—sure to evoke a mixed bag of emotions. Deep inside she dreaded the possibility that she would fall apart under the weight of her guilt.

Reagan looked up and threw a cursory glance around the terminal, her eyes breezing right past Heather at first and then flitting back and resting quizzically on her. Her lips parted, a confused frown forming. Heather smiled to let her know it was her, and, before she knew it, Reagan was wrapping her arms around her in a stiff embrace.

"It's good to see you again, Heather." Reagan pulled back, and appraised her, gripping her by the shoulders. "It's just horrible what happened to our poor Lindsay. I'm sure you're still in shock—we all are. I can't believe she's gone just like that—who would have thought? The whole community's reeling. People are scared to let their kids ride their bikes along the river. And of course the local news is sensationalizing it. They keep harping on about unusually aggressive snake activity this season. My daughter, Lucy, won't hardly go out to the garden by herself anymore."

Heather gave a sympathetic nod. "How old is Lucy?"

"Nine, going on nineteen," Reagan replied, rolling her eyes. "Dave teases her that she's going to save us a fortune on a college education because she already knows everything! Of course, being an only child, I will admit she's a bit spoiled..."

Heather let Reagan prattle on as they made their way out to the short-term parking lot. A wave of memories was surfing through her mind—picking up her grandparents at the airport when they came to visit, a trip to Disney World she and Violet had taken with their parents, and, of course, her farewell flight to LA twelve years earlier.

Reagan clicked her key fob and opened the hatchback on a white Subaru SUV.

"Would you mind if we called to visit Lindsay's mom on the way?" Heather asked.

"Pam went to stay with her sister and brother-in-law for a few weeks," Reagan answered, gesturing for Heather's bag. "I don't think she had much choice. They insisted on taking her back with them."

Heather frowned. "Where do they live?"

"Sioux City." Reagan threw her a calculating look. "You won't have time to drive up there and back before the reunion tomorrow night if that's what you're thinking. Maybe you could extend your ticket and drive up on Monday instead."

"I have to be back in LA Sunday night. I have a case I'm working on," Heather explained. "It was all I could do to take the weekend off."

Reagan twisted her lips in a disapproving manner as she started up the car. "Well, at least you made it back for the reunion."

On the drive, they fell into uneasy conversation, catching each other up on their lives, and tossing around a few ideas for paying tribute to Lindsay at the reunion. Before long, they were pulling into the driveway of a modest brick home on a street lined with Dogwood trees. A smattering of reddish leaves dotted the asphalt hinting at the impending fall finale to come.

"Pretty area you live in," Heather commented as she climbed out of the car.

A flicker of irritation crossed Reagan's face before she answered. "It's convenient—a twenty-minute drive to my office. Dave and I moved here after we got married."

"I'm looking forward to meeting him," Heather said.

"You'll be glad to know he's nothing like Lucy's deadbeat

biological father," Reagan answered. "He adopted her shortly after we got married."

Heather bit her lip. She had never understood why Reagan had wasted years of her life on that loser, Roy Krueger. He'd refused to marry her, even after Lucy was born. And, from what Heather had gathered from Lindsay over the years, he was a shady character, always between jobs.

The front door swung open as they walked up the steps and a young girl with thick, dark ringlets and huge, brown eyes peered out at them.

"This is my daughter, Lucy," Reagan said.

Heather pulled off her sunglasses and smiled at her. "Nice to meet you. I'm Heather."

"Hello," Lucy responded warily, before stepping aside to let her in.

"You can leave your bags in the hall for now," Reagan said. "I'll introduce you to Dave." Without waiting for a response, she strode down the hallway. "Honey? Where are you?"

"In the kitchen," a baritone voice called back.

Heather followed Reagan into a French country style kitchen with a collection of ceramic roosters atop cream-colored cabinetry. Her mouth watered at the garlic-infused tomato sauce aroma that greeted her. A slim, salt-and-pepper-haired man was stirring a large pot on the stove top. When they entered, he set down his ladle on the spoon rest and wiped his hands on the towel hanging from his waist. "You must be Heather." He extended a hand. "Welcome to our home. I'm Dave."

She shook his hand, noting the firm grip and the friendly eyes that met hers. She had been shocked to hear that Reagan was getting married only a year after ending her relationship with Roy, but it seemed she had finally found herself a decent man.

"Hope you're hungry," Dave said. "I'm making a big pot of spaghetti Bolognese." He gave her a disarming wink. "The girls tell me it's my specialty—personally, I think my dance moves are more impressive than my cooking."

Heather chuckled. "It smells delicious. It has to be better than the leftovers I usually exist on."

"Come on, let's take your bag up to your room and get you settled in," Reagan said.

Heather followed her upstairs and into a light and airy guest room at the back of the house. "Great view," she remarked, looking out over the lawn and manicured shrubbery to the open fields and trees beyond.

"Yes, we're lucky," Reagan agreed. "The house backs up to a park, so we'll always have an unobstructed vista."

Heather flinched as it suddenly hit her all over again why she was here. "I was hoping we could drive out to the Great River Trail this evening."

Reagan threw her an alarmed look. "Tonight? I mean ... we could go in the morning."

"I won't be able to sleep unless I see where it happened," Heather said. "It doesn't seem real yet. I need closure before the reunion."

Reagan gave a dubious nod. "Okay. I'll leave you to get unpacked. Come on down whenever you're ready."

Heather unzipped her case and hung up her outfit for the reunion—black pants and a sleeveless black silk shirt—before freshening up in the bathroom.

Dinner was an awkward affair with Reagan presiding over the conversation—waxing lyrical about her grandiose plans for the reunion. Heather was relieved when Dave rose from the table and began clearing away the dishes. "If you ladies are still planning on driving out to the trail you should go now before it gets dark. Lucy and I will clean up the kitchen."

"Thanks Dave. That was delicious," Heather said as she got to her feet. "I can't speak for your dancing, but your Bolognese lives up to its reputation."

REAGAN PARKED her Subaru along the road near an entrance to the Great River Trail and unbuckled her seatbelt. "I'll show you where they found her. It's only a few hundred feet from here. They had the area taped off, but it's open again now. The wreaths might still be there."

"If you don't mind, I'd rather go alone," Heather said. "I won't be long. I just need a few minutes to ... talk to Lindsay."

Reagan arched an annoyed brow. "As you wish."

Heather climbed out of the car and walked briskly along the trail, hands shoved deep into her pockets, praying she didn't bump into anyone she knew. The temperature was dropping but the fall foliage was in full bloom, warming her heart with memories of stomping through leaves as a child. A wave of grief hit with unexpected force when she spotted the wilting floral tribute up ahead. Her heart felt like someone was kneading it like dough. She slowed her pace to allow a jogger, who'd stopped at the makeshift memorial, time to move on. As soon as he resumed his run, she took a deep breath and made her way over to the wreaths. She hunkered down next to them and began reading the attached cards and notes. Several were names she recognized. Tears dampened her eyes as she whispered a few words to Lindsay letting her know how much she regretted allowing their friendship to wane over the years.

When she was done, she got to her feet and walked around behind the display. A tiny piece of yellow caution tape tied around a tree trunk fluttered in the evening breeze. Heather walked over to examine it. Her eyes settled on a large nearby rock. She stuffed her hands back into her pockets and kicked at it in frustration. It was so horribly unfair—this should never have happened to someone as kind and accomplished as Lindsay. She turned aside and stomped deeper into the brush, trying not to scream her frustration aloud. It wasn't as if she hadn't encountered the randomness of death before in her line of work. But this was personal.

Blinking through her tears, she caught sight of something glinting up at her in the evening sun. She kicked at the brush half-heartedly trying to identify it. Pulling one hand out of her pocket, she bent over and retrieved it. A stainless steel hook, about two inches long, attached to a threaded plastic handle that was cracked at the base. She turned it over, unsure of its purpose. It wasn't a bike part, and it was too big to be a tool from Lindsay's repair kit.

A cold shiver traversed Heather's shoulders as a disturbing thought struck her. Was it a coincidence that she'd found the hook so close to the spot where Lindsay had crashed? Or was it possible someone had used it as a trap—to catch the wheel of her bike?

4

The following afternoon, Reagan tucked her arm into Heather's as they walked up to the marquee in the hotel foyer welcoming the North Valley High class of 1998.

"Just as well you decided to come," Reagan quipped. "I wouldn't have had a date if it hadn't been for you."

Lucy had come down with a fever at the last minute and Dave had volunteered to stay home with her. Truth be told, Heather thought he looked more relieved than disappointed at the prospect of missing the reunion. She suspected he was tired of hearing Reagan droning on about it and dreading the introductions she had lined up for him. Playing Reagan's sidekick was not an enviable role.

"It's too bad Dave couldn't be here," Heather replied, disengaging herself from Reagan's grip.

"I was so looking forward to introducing him to everyone," Reagan answered with a dramatic sigh. "But I couldn't have found a babysitter at such short notice, and there's no way *I* can miss the reunion as chair of the planning committee."

Heather stretched a polite smile over her lips. Reagan hadn't changed much—never missing an opportunity to let everyone know how important she was.

As soon as they stepped inside the banquet room reserved for the event, Reagan began flitting around fussing with decorations and directing the hotel staff to make last-minute adjustments to the layout. They had arrived three hours early, which Heather suspected might exasperate the staff who were still setting up. But Reagan had wanted to make sure there were no eleventh-hour glitches to her meticulous plans.

"So, what do you think? Looks amazing, doesn't it?" she remarked, beaming at Heather as she finished laying out the name tags on the check-in table. "Josh and I came up with the *Better With Age* theme. We have charcuterie platters with aged cheeses from all around the world. And we're serving wine that's the same vintage as our graduation year."

"Somebody say my name?"

Heather spun around to see Josh Halverson striding toward them. He'd filled out a little since high school, and there were a few telltale grays sprouting up around his temples, but he was still a strikingly handsome man with the kind of smile that generally greased the way in life.

"Well, look who's back in town!" he said, walking straight up to Heather and embracing her. "Good to see you again. I'm so sorry about Lindsay. You were closer to her than any of us, but we're all gutted over it."

Heather took a ragged breath, fighting a rogue wave of emotion. "It was so unexpected ... and gruesome."

Josh gave a weighty nod. "Lindsay would be glad you came tonight." He ran his eyes over her slim frame. "You look great, by the way. That LA lifestyle must agree with you. All that sunshine, I suppose."

Heather gave a wry grin. "I'm on the vampire shift. I mostly work nights—surveillance type stuff—and sleep during the day."

Josh regarded her with a mock contemplative air. "And you're dressed all in black—maybe you really are a vampire. Guess we'll find out as the night progresses."

Heather laughed self-consciously. Was he flirting with her or was she reading too much into it?

"Josh has weathered the years pretty well himself, don't you think?" Reagan gushed, digging her nails into his arm as she snuggled up next to him. "Keep him in mind if you have any single gal pals in LA looking to date a hot doctor."

Josh cleared his throat, looking uncomfortable. "You probably heard that Ally and I split?"

"Yes. I'm sorry," Heather said. "I was surprised to hear that, to be honest. High school sweethearts and all."

Josh gave a disheartened shrug. "It was best we parted ways. She cheated on me with a colleague, and things were never the same after that. We kept bickering over the stupidest things, taking separate vacations—doing everything people in healthy relationships don't do. But enough of that depressing topic. Let's focus on tonight."

"What do you think of the set up?" Reagan cut in, gesturing to the sea of round tables with white floor-length tablecloths, black napkins, and silver candelabras glinting under the lights strung around the room. "I did a quick walk around and everything looks good."

"Thanks to your ninja organizational skills," Josh said. "Where's your beau tonight?"

Reagan pulled a face. "Lucy's sick. Dave stayed home with her." She glanced at her watch and let out a gasp.

"We'd better get busy unloading my car. The prizes for the games are on the back seat. Josh, you can help me carry in the gift bags. Heather, put a pen and a button at each place setting." She pointed to a small plastic tub on the check-in table. "Everything's in there."

Heather lifted out one of the buttons and read the message aloud. "*Hi, I can't remember your name either.*" She let out a snort. "Sounds like we're hosting a dementia convention."

"They're intended as an ice breaker," Reagan retorted, cutting her a sharp glare. "Put one of the bingo cards on each chair too. Marco and Sydney should be here any minute to help."

Heather carried the box of buttons and bingo sheets to the front of the room and began working her way back through the tables. Reagan ran around directing traffic in her usual high-handed manner—a good reminder of why Heather hadn't missed her in the past twelve years. On the other hand, seeing Josh again had stirred up some unexpected feelings. She hoped he hadn't found her too standoffish. She was trying to be sociable, but the truth was her thoughts weren't on the reunion. Being here had brought the reality of Lindsay's death home. And her investigator brain was in overdrive. The hook she had found in the brush gnawed at her. Experience told her things like that were rarely coincidences.

At the sound of footsteps, she lifted her head expecting to see Reagan and Josh returning with the prizes.

"Heather! You made it!" a stocky, dark-haired man called to her.

She set down the tub of supplies and greeted him. "Marco! It's good to see you again."

He gestured to the portly woman at his side stuffed into

an unflattering grape-colored silk cocktail dress. "This is my wife, Anna."

Anna held out a hand embellished with an assortment of expensive-looking rings. A glittering tennis bracelet slid down her wrist. "I've heard all about you. You're the celebrity PI from LA."

Heather shook her hand, acknowledging the compliment with an abashed smile. "I make a decent living, but no movie deals yet."

Marco raised a dark, shaggy brow. "I didn't expect you to come. Guess we have to die before you show up."

"Marco!" Anna hissed at him reprovingly. "Leave it alone." She turned to Heather. "I'm sorry. This thing with Lindsay has messed him up."

"Don't worry about it," Heather reassured her. "It's messed us all up."

"Hey, gang!" a female voice called from across the room.

Heather peered over her shoulder to see Sydney tottering into the room on four-inch heels, an elegant-looking man in a sports coat hovering protectively at her side.

"No way!" Sydney exclaimed. "Heather's here!" She minced over to her and enveloped her in a flimsy hug. Heather wrinkled her nose at the overpowering scent of perfume.

"Reagan said you were planning on coming, but I didn't really believe you would show." Sydney motioned to the man at her side. "This is my husband, Steve."

They shook hands and exchanged a few pleasantries before Reagan barged back into the room, brandishing a clipboard. Josh was hard on her heels, pushing a cart laden down with gift bags, one-handedly attempting to hold the precarious load in place.

"Great, everyone's here now," Reagan chirped. "Gather round and I'll go over the tribute to Lindsay."

Sydney cocked an amused brow and whispered to Heather, "Bossy as ever, isn't she?"

"Parks and Rec has given us permission to plant a tree and erect a small memorial plaque along the trail in Lindsay's memory," Reagan began. "I'm going to announce it right before dinner, then show a short tribute video and ask for a moment of silence. I figured it would be more respectful to do it at the beginning of the evening rather than at the end after everyone's been drinking and hollering. Besides, I don't want to end the night on a downer." She reached into her oversized purse and pulled out some paper-clipped sheets. "This is the list of games I've selected. I'm counting on all of you to help me hand out any props needed, as well as to welcome people as they arrive, direct traffic—that type of thing. Any questions?"

"Looks like you've got it all figured out, as usual," Marco said. "Let's grab a cocktail and toast Lindsay."

As the room began to fill up, Heather found herself mingling with her former classmates and catching up on lives she knew next to nothing about—full and varied lives, littered with weddings, births, and growing families. Everything she had missed out on—held out on, if she was being honest. Over it all, hung the cloud of Lindsay's untimely demise. It was just so shocking and bizarre. Inevitably, every conversation turned to it at some point. *If only she hadn't gone biking alone. They ought to have more park security on the trails. Her poor mother. My kids are having nightmares about rattlesnakes. They say our county has an infestation problem.*

Heather dutifully made her rounds among the tables, clutching a club soda and cranberry. Alcohol had played a pivotal role in what had happened to Violet that night, and

Heather had never had any desire to partake of it since. Besides, her PI job required her to keep a clear head—she never knew when she might have to jump in her car and conduct a last-minute surveillance assignment.

Once everyone had taken their seats, Reagan picked up the mic and officially kicked off the evening by welcoming everyone. After sharing her plan for a tribute tree and memorial plaque, she raised a glass to toast their fallen classmate. The room fell silent as they viewed a short slideshow featuring high school pictures of Lindsay and more recent shots of her holding up trophies as she sat astride her bike, her racing helmet fastened beneath her chin.

Heather bit back tears as she glanced across at the empty chair they had left at their table to honor Lindsay. She should be there with them. It was all wrong—all wrong like the hook Heather had found near the trail and tucked away in her suitcase. Something about the accident didn't sit right with her. Could it have been deliberate—teenagers messing around? Trying to trip someone up for the fun of it, a dare gone horribly wrong? Or something more sinister?

"All right, everyone," Reagan crooned into the mic, "Let's get things rolling with our first game of the evening: *Team Jeopardy!*"

Before long, the atmosphere became more jovial and the crowd grew more raucous as they competed to answer trivia questions from 1998, yelling out song titles to match video clips on the screen overhead, and racing around the room trying to pair baby photos to their classmates.

"I think it's going well, don't you?" Reagan said, beaming proudly around their table.

"Everyone seems to be having a blast," Josh agreed.

"The photo booth with the 1998 wardrobe and the wigs

is a huge hit," Sydney chimed in. "I posted a few pics to Facebook already."

"Food's not bad either," Marco remarked, apprising the half-eaten plate of succulent steak, seared asparagus and garlic mashed potatoes in front of him.

"That's a winning endorsement, coming from you," Josh said.

Reagan turned to Heather. "Did you know that Marco owns three restaurants now: The Sardinian, Bella Calabria, and Veneto?" She reached over and grabbed Anna's hand. "See all those rings? Marco's culinary skills paid for every last one of them."

Anna smiled stiffly as she jerked her hand away.

Heather threw a furtive look at Marco. Judging by the dark expression on his face, he hadn't missed the barbed tone in Reagan's compliment. What was that all about?

Heather glanced up as a waiter approached carrying an enormous floral arrangement of delicate blue flowers.

"Delivery for the student council table," he announced. He set the flowers down with a flourish and scurried off, his face gleaming with sweat.

"How thoughtful!" Reagan preened. "Someone must want to thank me for all the hard work I put in organizing the reunion."

"Those are forget-me-nots," Sydney said, rubbing a petal between her fingers. "Unusual choice for a flower arrangement. I wonder who it's from."

"Let's find out." Reagan reached for the attached envelope, slipped the card out, and gasped.

5

Reagan dropped the card on the table and pressed her trembling fingers to her lips.

Heather laid a hand on her arm. "What is it? What's wrong?"

"Tell us what the card says!" Sydney demanded.

Reagan gulped, her face washed out and pale beneath her carefully applied make up. Wordlessly, she slid the card across the table. Sydney snatched it up and read it aloud. "*You deserve to die!*" She frowned and turned it over. "That's rich! This has got to be some kind of sick joke."

Heather darted a glance around the room on the off chance she might catch someone watching their shocked reactions with a satisfied smirk on their face, but everyone appeared to be engaged in conversations of their own, oblivious to the drama unfolding at their table.

Marco held out his hand for the card, studying it with a scowl before tossing it aside. "My guess is it's someone who had it in for the student council back in the day. Didn't like all the power we had." He looked directly at Reagan. "Let's face it, you rubbed a lot of people the wrong way."

She shot him an indignant glare. "Are you saying this is my fault?"

He glowered back at her. "You need to chill, it's just a prank. Someone's trying to wind us up, and you're falling for it." He glanced around the room. "They're probably splitting their sides right now, telling the rest of their table not to look over here. Ignore the card. Don't let them rattle you."

"Easier said than done," Josh chimed in. "It's a tough message to ignore." He turned to Heather. "You're the investigative expert. What do you think?"

Heather cleared her throat, selecting her words with care. She was thinking a lot of things—like maybe someone had deliberately caused Lindsay's biking accident and was trying to intimidate the rest of the student council too for some inexplicable reason. If Lindsay's death had been a prank gone wrong, then it was unlikely the card was connected to it. But what if someone had wanted Lindsay dead—wanted them all dead? As shocking a thought as it was, there was no denying the fact that the message read like a threat: *you deserve to die.* Who did *you* refer to? All of them, or one of them?

"Heather?" Josh was peering at her, his brows scrunched together.

"Sorry! My PI instincts are in overdrive. I was thinking through all the possibilities," she said. "I agree with Marco. It's most likely one of the other clubs yanking our chain. Let's face it, we weren't popular with everyone. Granted, it's in extremely poor taste, considering what happened to Lindsay, but maybe someone set up the flower order before her accident and forgot to cancel it."

"People need to get a life," Sydney huffed. "This isn't the least bit funny. I feel like reporting it to the police."

"They're not going to do anything about it," Marco

scoffed. "A prank flower delivery at a class reunion isn't exactly a high priority weekend call for the cops."

"I wonder what the significance of the forget-me-nots is," Anna mused, tapping a polished fingernail on the table as she studied the floral arrangement.

"Maybe someone's letting us know they haven't forgotten what we did to tick them off," Josh said. "Although I've no idea what that could be."

"Could be anything," Marco added. "It was one drama after another back in the day." He fired another dark look Reagan's way as he reached for his wine glass.

Heather scanned the room again. It was possible this was nothing more than a tactless practical joke. As class president, Reagan had been overbearing in the way she handled things—steamrolling over anyone who stood in her way. And it never ceased to amaze Heather how long some people could harbor grudges. Still, it was particularly vindictive, considering the fact that tonight had been dedicated to Lindsay's memory.

"We need to get to the bottom of it," Sydney said. "It makes me uncomfortable to think there are people out there who hate us to this very day."

"It shouldn't be too hard to track down the company that delivered the flowers," her husband, Steve, piped up.

Heather nodded. "That's the easy part. But there's no guarantee the florist will have a record of who placed the order. They could have paid in cash."

Reagan furrowed her brow. "I could grab the mic right now and ask who sent it—pretend we want to thank them. Maybe I can embarrass them into admitting to the stunt and force them to apologize publicly."

Josh smoothed a hand over his jaw, looking decidedly uncomfortable. "That's probably not the best way to handle it. You'll completely kill the atmosphere you've worked so hard to create. And what if no one admits to it? That would be even more awkward. Everyone will be viewing each other with suspicion. That's all they'll talk about for the rest of the evening, *if* they even stay after that. Besides, we don't know for sure that someone here was behind it."

Sydney threw him an alarmed look. "Who else could it have been?" She glanced around the table in bewilderment.

"Josh is right," Heather said. "We can't stand up and accuse someone here of pulling this stunt without being sure of our facts. We're only going to tick off a lot of people."

Marco picked the card back up and flicked his nail against it. "*You deserve to die.* Is that all of us or one of us? What if this has nothing to do with high school? I'm willing to bet we've all ticked people off since then."

"It could be a disgruntled employee," Anna interjected. "You've had a few troublemakers."

"The question is, what are we going to do about it?" Sydney asked.

"I can raise the matter in a follow up email after the reunion," Reagan suggested. "Maybe someone will respond."

"Or we could simply ignore it," Marco said.

Josh nodded. "As disturbing as it is, it's most likely a prank. I vote to ignore it. Don't give the moron behind it the satisfaction of a reaction."

He looked around the table expectantly. One by one, the others nodded in dubious assent. Heather did likewise, but she snapped a quick picture of the handwriting on the card, nonetheless. She didn't want to needlessly fan the flames of fear. But she couldn't ignore the message entirely. Just like she couldn't ignore the hook. She didn't know how, but her instincts told her the two were connected.

6

B ack in LA, Heather threw herself into her work with renewed vigor. After wrapping up her surveillance duties for Karan Patel, she sent him a hefty invoice for the juicy evidence of his wife's extra-marital shenanigans. If nothing else, it would ensure that the gold-digging, party-hopping, substantially younger, and soon-to-be-ex Mrs. Patel wouldn't walk away with half the fortune Karan's decades of hard work and ingenuity had amassed.

In between cases, Heather had taken the time to contact her sister, Violet, and asked her to make a few inquiries at local florists back in Iowa. She had been able to nail down the business that had fulfilled the order for the forget-me-not arrangement and delivered it to the reunion. But, as Heather had suspected, the customer had paid in cash. The florist was unable to give Violet much of a description other than that it was a woman with long, brown hair and glasses —either or both of which could easily have been part of a disguise. The woman might even have been hired to place the order on someone else's behalf. Heather had reluctantly retired the whole unsettling affair to the back burner while she focused on more pressing matters that paid the bills.

She was returning home from a rare trip to the grocery store one morning when her phone rang. Reagan's number came up on the screen. She placed her bag of groceries on the kitchen counter and perched on a barstool, with Phoebe in her lap, to take the call.

"Hey Reagan, how's it go—"

"Someone tried to kill Marco last night!" Reagan blurted out. "They set fire to one of his restaurants!"

Heather stiffened, pressing the phone tight to her ear, while ruffling Phoebe's ears. "Are you sure it was arson?"

Reagan gulped back a sob and continued talking, seemingly oblivious to the question. "And two days ago, someone cut me off on the freeway. They tried to kill me too! I knew we should have taken the card at the reunion seriously. It was a real threat. I should have confronted everyone that night. We shouldn't have let them get away with it. I'm telling you, one of our former classmates is a psycho."

"Okay, calm down and take a breath," Heather soothed, slipping into professional mode. "Let's talk this through. Which restaurant was it?"

"Bella Calabria. It's on the west side of town."

"How do you know the fire wasn't accidental?"

"The fire investigator found accelerant at the scene. He said it was definitely arson—an amateur. Apparently, they didn't make much of an attempt to hide their tracks."

Heather rubbed a hand over her temples digesting this information. "Maybe Anna was right that Marco has a disgruntled employee."

"But what about me?" Reagan cried. "Someone's after me as well. I almost crashed when they cut me off. Everyone on the freeway was laying on their horns."

"Did you get a look at the driver?"

"Not really. It all happened so fast. I was concentrating on trying not to hit anyone."

Heather thought for a moment. "Could you tell if it was a man or a woman?"

"No, they were wearing a hoodie—probably trying to hide their face."

"We can't be sure the two events are connected," Heather said, trying not to sound overly dismissive of Reagan's fears. "I get cut off on LA freeways almost every day. The arson is another matter. Let's focus on that. Did Marco tell the police about the flower delivery at the reunion?"

"Yes. Thankfully, I kept the card. I turned it over to the police. They want to do some kind of handwriting analysis on it."

The gears in Heather's brain were whirring. Evidently, the police thought the possibility of the threatening message and the arson being connected had some merit. But it would take time to compare the handwriting on the card to that of everyone who had attended the class reunion. Even if the police followed through on it, there was no guarantee they would find a match. Still, it was worth a shot. It was the only potential lead they had.

"I've been thinking it over," Reagan rambled on. "There is another possibility. I'm worried Roy—my ex—might be behind it."

Heather rubbed her fingers across her brow. "What makes you say that?"

"I got custody of Lucy after we split. He was furious about it. He swore he'd get even with me. I haven't heard anything from him in a while, but it's possible he's been plotting all this time."

"I doubt he'd take the risk of causing a wreck in front of

potential witnesses," Heather responded. "In my experience, violent exes are far more likely to wait in a dark alley
or break into a woman's house at night when she's all alone
and defenseless, cowards that they are."

"You don't know Roy like I do," Reagan said, with a
tremor in her voice. "Road rage is right up his alley."

"It still doesn't explain the arson," Heather countered.
"What reason would Roy have to target Marco?"

For a long moment, there was silence on the other end
of the line.

Heather puckered her forehead. "Reagan? Are you still
there?"

"Yes. Just trying to think, that's all. I don't know why Roy
does what he does. He doesn't act rationally when he's been
drinking. Maybe he was trying to lash out at me by hurting
my friends."

"Did you share your concerns with the police?"

There was another long pause before Reagan
responded. "I can't. I don't know for sure if Roy's behind it. If
he finds out I went to the police, he might come after me, or
Lucy."

Alarm bells were going off in Heather's head. Reagan
was skirting around her questions. There was something
she wasn't telling her—some connection between Marco
and Roy that Reagan didn't want her to know about. Were
they acquainted with each other? And if so, how? It's not like
they went to the same school. Heather couldn't picture them
socializing together. From what she'd gathered, Roy hadn't
liked Reagan getting together with her old school friends.

"Isn't there something you can do to get to the bottom of
it?" Reagan asked. "I can pay you for your time."

"It's not about the money," Heather answered. "I just
don't think there's much I can add to what's already being

done. The police are investigating the arson and you're only speculating that someone deliberately cut you off on the freeway. You're making an assumption that two random events have an underlying connection."

"You don't understand," Reagan protested. "They *are* connected."

"How can you be so sure?" Heather asked. "Is there something you're not telling me? I can't help you if you're not being honest with me."

Reagan cleared her throat. "This is really ... difficult. I'm taking a huge risk. I need you to promise me you won't breathe a word of this to the others—or to anyone else, for that matter."

Heather's brain blared an inner warning. It was happening again. A pact to keep a dirty little secret. Just like she'd promised to keep Lindsay's. She didn't want the responsibility—or the emotional baggage that went along with it. What could Reagan possibly have to tell her that she didn't want to share with the others? Did Marco and Roy have some kind of long-standing rift? Perhaps Marco had fired Roy at some point. Heather had never actually met Roy Krueger, but, by all accounts, he was a powder keg of anger. And Marco could get riled up and lose his temper in half a heartbeat too. Maybe they'd gotten into a physical altercation. After deliberating for a moment or two, she said, "I can promise you this, I won't say anything to the others so long as it's not detrimental to them."

"It has nothing to do with them," Reagan insisted. "But for Marco's sake, Josh and Sydney can't find out what I'm about to tell you."

Heather shifted Phoebe's position in her lap, growing more intrigued by the minute. Had Marco done something illegal—beaten Roy up or threatened him? That would certainly explain why Reagan didn't want to go to the police.

"It was years ago," Reagan began, her voice small and wistful. "I was in a bad spot. Roy was abusive from the start of our relationship, but I hid it from everyone. Sometimes, when I needed to get out of the house, I would go to Marco's restaurant—he only had one location back then. He'd let me sit at a little table near the kitchen. On slow nights, he'd join me, crack open a bottle of wine and ask me how things were going. I began to open up to him. I told him how abusive Roy was." She dragged out a heavy breath. "He offered to take care of him for me—nothing too drastic. Just send a couple of guys around to rough him up and warn him not to touch me again."

Heather traced her nails lightly across her forehead, trying to figure out where this was going. If Marco had assaulted Roy, it was too late now to press charges. But maybe Roy, fired up at losing custody of his daughter, had decided to even that old score with Marco and get back at Reagan in a roundabout sort of way. If he couldn't hurt her, he would hurt her friends.

"Of course, I begged Marco not to. I told him I didn't want him getting involved," Reagan continued. "Trying to intimidate Roy would only have enraged him more. Marco said the offer was always on the table if I ever changed my mind. That night, over a couple of bottles of wine, he shared his struggles with his own marriage. He said he and Anna had drifted apart. She was only interested in the kids, and she'd put on a lot of weight and quit working out which bothered him, even though he felt like a heel for thinking that way, and he didn't dare bring it up with her."

Heather stared down at the gleaming white tiles on her kitchen floor, her heart pounding. A sixth sense told her what was coming next. The prelude to an admission to infidelity always took the same course—a suitably subdued tone, tinged with an air of regret, punctuated with delicate pauses.

"I know it's cliché to say it, but one thing led to another." Reagan's voice grew quiet. "We had this emotional connection, the kind that only two people in pain can really understand."

"Cut to the chase, Reagan. Are you telling me you had an affair with Marco?" Heather asked.

"It was more of a fling," Reagan answered sheepishly. "We both regretted it afterward. He begged me not to tell Anna. He was afraid she would divorce him, and he didn't want to see his kids' lives torn apart."

"And you think Roy found out about your *fling*, as you call it?" Heather prompted.

"Yes—or maybe he knew all along. Setting fire to Marco's restaurant is another way of punishing me for the affair, and for taking Lucy away from him. That's what this is about—the threatening card, the arson, cutting me off on the freeway. Roy won't rest until he kills me."

7

Heather lay curled up on the couch with Phoebe in her lap. A mug of lukewarm tea sat on the coffee table in front of her. She had been replaying her conversation with Reagan over in her head for hours, deconstructing it to figure out what it was that she was missing. Reagan had seemed genuinely afraid that Roy might come after her. But her story didn't add up. A man with anger issues as deep as Roy's wouldn't keep quiet about Reagan's affair all these years. And if he'd only just found out about it, he'd be far more likely to swing a punch and leave her with a black eye than send her a bouquet with a cryptic message.

Phoebe stirred in her sleep making a snuffling sound like a newborn. When Heather had first got her at only eight-weeks-old, the noise had scared her. She'd thought Phoebe was struggling to breathe. But the vet had assured her the snorting noises were all part and parcel of a Shih tzu's genetic makeup—that flat nose and pushed-in face that Heather loved coming home to more than anything, or anyone, in the world. It was hard for her to trust people after what happened to Violet. Her wariness had served her well in her career, but it had done nothing for her relationships. She stroked her hand gently over Phoebe's silky head and then took a tentative sip of her tea before setting it back down with a grunt of disgust. It had cooled beyond the point of redemption.

Reaching for her phone, she scrolled through her contacts for Marco's number. She hesitated for only a moment before dialing. There was no way around it. She had to feel him out and see if he suspected Roy was behind the arson too. After the fourth ring, he picked up.

"Hi, Marco. Just checking in," she said. "I heard about the fire. No one hurt, I hope?"

"No. Thankfully, all the employees had already left for the night."

"How bad's the damage?"

"Hard to say. The adjuster's still assessing it. The fire department managed to put it out before the whole place burned down. It's a big blow though. It will be weeks before I can reopen. I've had to furlough most of my employees at that location."

"Any idea who was behind it?" Heather asked.

"I can't think of anyone who has a big enough beef with me to burn down my building."

"A disgruntled ex-employee, maybe? Anna mentioned you've had a few of them."

Marco grunted. "It's been months since I fired anyone. I had this one employee a few years back who claimed he got injured on the job and ended up suing me. He lost the case, but it's hard to believe he would take it this far. And why now? I passed his contact information on to the police anyway. How did you find out about the fire?"

"Reagan called me. She's all in a tizzy—she's convinced it's connected to what happened at the reunion."

"So she thinks the threatening message was intended for me?" Marco asked, sounding incredulous.

"Not exactly. She thinks she's being targeted too. Someone cut her off on the freeway the other day. She's worried they were trying to kill her."

Marco said nothing for a few minutes. Heather could hear him breathing on the other end of the line.

"I told her I didn't think it had anything to do with the arson at your restaurant," she continued. "That was more likely to be a revengeful employee or something. But for some reason she's got it in her head that Roy is behind everything."

"Why? Has he been bothering her?" Marco asked, his tone unusually sharp.

"Apparently he was furious when she got custody of Lucy and he swore he'd get even." Heather allowed a thoughtful pause to unfold before adding in a questioning tone, "Of course, that doesn't explain the arson, unless Roy had a reason to target you too?"

Marco huffed out a rough breath. "She told you, didn't she? About us."

"Yes," Heather admitted. "She asked me to investigate what was going on and find out if Roy was behind it. I told her I wouldn't consider it unless she was honest with me about why she thought Roy was targeting you as well. She made me promise not to tell Sydney or Josh about your affair."

"Look, it should never have happened—me and Reagan. It was stupid. We were both in a bad spot at the time. Anna doesn't know about it and it needs to stay that way. We're getting on fine now, but if it comes out, Anna will leave me. You have no idea what that would do to my kids."

"That's between you and Anna," Heather responded.

"Good enough." Marco answered gruffly. "So, are you going to look into this? The police are investigating the arson, but they have no leads. If you're willing to come back to Iowa and take this on as an assignment, I'll cough up the dough for your services."

"Thanks, Marco, but like I told Reagan, this isn't about the money," Heather replied. "I just don't see any clear connection yet—not enough to merit an investigation. Some idiot probably pranked us at the reunion. A ticked off employee might very well have set fire to the restaurant. As for somebody cutting Reagan off on the freeway—it happens every day. She's overreacting."

"You might be right, but we don't know for sure, do we? There could be more to it than that. Will you at least think about it?"

"I will, but I'm not making any promises."

"That's all I'm asking. I'll give you a jingle in a couple of days," Marco said before hanging up.

Heather sank back on the couch and closed her eyes. Despite downplaying it with Marco, she couldn't rule out the possibility that there was some connection between the unsettling incidents. But the bigger question in her mind was whether any of this had to do with Lindsay's untimely death.

She had just nodded off when her phone rang again. Groaning, she slid her finger across the screen and took the call.

"Did you hear what happened?" Sydney gasped, dispensing with any opening pleasantries.

Heather unwound herself from the awkward position

she'd been sleeping in and massaged her neck. "If you mean the fire at Bella Calabria, then yes. I talked to Marco a little while ago."

"I'm freaking out, Heather," Sydney blathered on. "That flower delivery's been haunting me ever since the reunion. It was a real threat. Reagan told me someone almost killed her on the freeway the other day. Which of us is next on the hit list? Steve's beside himself—he's worried sick about my safety. You need to get back here and investigate this."

"I don't think we should get ahead of ourselves," Heather said in an overly patient tone. "Marco told me he had a disgruntled employee who sued him a while back. He passed his contact information on to the police. If it turns out he was behind the arson, then we can dismiss what happened at the reunion as a prank. As for Reagan getting cut off on the freeway, it's an everyday occurrence—you can't read too much into that."

"But what if some psycho is targeting us?" Sydney ranted. "I don't want to end my days as an episode of Unsolved Mysteries."

Heather suppressed a chuckle, trying to convey an understanding note when she answered, "Let's wait and hear what the police say after interviewing Marco's ex-employee. If he turns out to be the *psycho* as you put it, he'll be prosecuted, and this will all be over." Heather glanced at the time on her phone. "Listen, I have to go, Sydney. I have a job I'm supposed to be on. We'll talk more once I hear back from Marco on the arson investigation."

After ending the call, Heather tossed her phone on the couch and ruffled Phoebe's neck absentmindedly. The only one of the group who hadn't tried to recruit her investigative services yet was Josh—the one person from whom she would have welcomed a call. Maybe it had something to do with the fact that he was a psychiatrist, but his calm demeanor made him easy to converse with. She needed someone to talk over the emotionally charged situation with in a rational manner, if nothing else.

After filling Phoebe's water bowl and giving her a treat, Heather pulled on her hat and coat and grabbed her backpack and camera. The assignment she was on tonight was a welcome diversion from the usual messy love triangles she specialized in. She had been hired to follow the sixteen-year-old son of two prominent LA lawyers. They had discovered drugs in his room and wanted to know where he was getting his supply, so they could squelch it without any repercussions to their son's future prospects.

Heather parked along the road near the kid's school where she had a good view of his yellow custom Jeep Grand Cherokee. When the bell rang to signal the end of classes, she pulled out the photo she'd been given, and slipped on her shades, keeping a sharp eye on the students streaming out across the parking lot. A good-looking kid with shaggy, dirty blond hair came strolling by with an entourage of giggling girls clutching textbooks to their chests. When he reached his jeep, he leaned casually against the driver's door and chatted with them for several minutes before waving them off and peeling out of the parking lot, music blaring, wholly unaware that he was being tailed.

Keeping a discreet distance, Heather followed the vehicle to the other side of town. The jeep turned down a seedy side street and slowed to a crawl before coming to a complete stop next to a huddle of young males in hoodies and dark glasses. The kid sprang out, slung a slim, black backpack over one shoulder, and greeted them with a fist bump. After throwing wary glances around, they disappeared together through a graffitied door in the building behind them. Heather set her camera back down on the passenger seat. Her clients were not going to like what she had to tell them. Based on what she'd observed so far, she suspected their son wasn't just using drugs—he was dealing them.

Fifteen minutes later, he reappeared with a noticeably bulging backpack. Heather quickly snapped a series of photos before starting up her car and slipping quietly out of view. Luckily for him, the little hooligan had parents who were influential lawyers. He was going to need them.

Back at her condo, she pulled into the parking garage and picked up her mail before making her way inside. Phoebe skidded across the tile to greet her, barking in excited circles.

"Hey munchkin!" Heather cooed, tossing her mail on the counter and kneeling down to tickle Phoebe's ears. The dog stuck her rear end up in the air and pushed down on her front paws, wagging her little tail delightedly. Heather laughed at her antics, her spirits instantly lifted. Phoebe gave the place some semblance of home.

After grabbing a bottle of water from the fridge, she sat down at the kitchen island to browse through her mail. Tossing aside the circulars and postcard advertisements, she flipped through a photography magazine before tackling the usual slew of end-of-month bills and statements. She was shuffling unenthusiastically through them when a small, pale blue envelope caught her eye. Frowning, she ripped it open and pulled out a linen-textured card with a watercolor of a bunch of forget-me-nots tied with a piece of burlap. Her heart raced as she opened it. The words inside blurred together.

Once a killer, always a killer.

8

Heather dropped the card on the counter and ran her trembling fingers through her hair. Someone knew! Someone had found out what she'd done! There was no other explanation. The delivery of flowers with its ominous message at the reunion hadn't been a practical joke to wind them up. And it wasn't a general threat. It was directed at her, and her alone. *You deserve to die!* The second card confirmed it. *Once a killer, always a killer.* Someone had discovered her secret. But how had they found out? Her frenzied thoughts collided with one another as she battled to make sense of it all. Who could be sending the threatening cards? And if Reagan's crazy ex, Roy, wasn't behind it, why had Marco's restaurant been set on fire? Was someone taunting her by targeting her friends as well?

Phoebe pattered across the floor and whined. Heather picked her up and carried her over to the couch. The dog wriggled into a nook beneath her arm, seeming to sense that she needed the comfort of her little body snuggled up next to her. She couldn't think straight. Her head was filled with static. There was only one explanation. Lindsay had broken her trust and told someone. Maybe she'd sworn them to secrecy, and now that she was dead, that person wanted to let Heather know that her secret wasn't buried in the grave with Lindsay. But what did this person want? The fact that they hadn't gone straight to the police seemed to suggest that blackmail might be an angle. If they had done a little digging, they would know she was a successful Hollywood PI. And greed was a powerful motivator.

Heather almost jumped out of her skin when her phone buzzed on the coffee table. She stared at the screen, hesitating to take the call when she saw that it was Reagan. She couldn't talk to her now—she wasn't sure she could keep her voice from trembling long enough to hold a conversation. After letting the call go to voicemail, she closed her eyes and rubbed her throbbing temples. She'd barely had time to catch her breath before her phone began ringing again. She eyed Reagan's name on the screen, debating what to do. Marco must have talked to her. Reagan was probably going to press her to come back to Iowa and investigate what was going on. Heather wasn't ready to rehash that conversation—she needed time to think first. But what if something else had happened—another suspicious incident? What if someone was hurt—Sydney, or Josh? She couldn't ignore their safety now that she knew they were being targeted because of her. Steeling herself, she pushed Phoebe gently aside and hit the speaker button on her phone, not trusting her shaking fingers to hold it. "Hey, Reagan!" Her voice sounded overly buoyant, stiff and artificial to a practiced ear. But Reagan was usually too self-absorbed to pick up on such nuances.

"Did you get one too?" Reagan sobbed into the phone.

A chill prickled over Heather's shoulders. "Get ... what exactly?"

"Another card," Reagan cried. "With a bouquet of forget-me-nots on the front. We all got one."

Heather sucked in a silent breath. Her thoughts flitted back-and-forth like bats at dusk—here one second and gone the next, elusive shadows that she couldn't control.

"There was a message inside: *Once a killer, always a killer,*" Reagan went on, sniffing back more tears.

All at once, Heather's thoughts were spinning in an entirely different direction. If everyone had got the same card, then maybe this wasn't about her, after all. Her troubled conscience had leapt to the worst possible conclusion —that Lindsay had betrayed her. "Yes, I got it too," Heather said quietly.

"I'm so scared. This person's a nutcase," Reagan ranted on. "It's a warning—they've killed before and they'll do it again. They already tried to kill me and Marco. We need to do something. We can't just wait around for the next attack to come."

Heather pulled at a broken nail distractedly, wincing as she ripped it off. Reagan was right. They couldn't dismiss the messages as a prank any longer. Someone extremely dangerous was targeting them.

"You're in this as deep as the rest of us," Reagan continued. "Dave says if you won't help us, he's going to hire his own investigator to get to the bottom of it. I had to talk him out of driving over to Roy's place and confronting him about the card."

Heather puckered her brow, taken aback. Dave's reaction seemed a bit extreme. But maybe, as the successor to a violent ex, he felt the need to prove himself as Reagan's protector. Emotions were running high. And that's when people got hurt.

"Okay, go ahead and set up a group call with the others

to discuss how we're going to handle this. We need to make sure we're all on the same page," Heather said. "I'm available now if everyone else is."

After ending the call, she got to her feet and began pacing back-and-forth across the floor of her condo trying to organize her thoughts. She needed to apply the same logic to this situation as she did to all her other cases. It was a whole lot easier to distance herself when she wasn't emotionally invested, but she was a professional, after all. She knew how to put her game face on and roll up her sleeves.

There were two main questions to be answered right off the bat. The first was who the messages were intended for. And the second was whether they were connected to the arson. For now, she was going to set the freeway incident aside and chalk it up to another stressed-out driver having a bad day.

Her phone trilled with an incoming FaceTime call. Heather sat down at the counter, turned her phone sideways and studied the photo tiles of Reagan, Josh, and Sydney as they popped up on the screen one-by-one. Reagan's eyes were red rimmed from crying. The ordinarily animated Sydney appeared pale without her usual full face of makeup. Josh looked as if he'd just woken up from a nap, hair standing on end like Pampas grass, dressed in a wrinkled cotton T-shirt. Seconds later, Marco's image appeared on the screen, bobbing in and out of his square. He was evidently walking somewhere and trying to look at the camera at the same time. "Give me a minute," he said, sounding flustered. "I'm at The Sardinian—can't hear a thing. We're slammed now that one of our locations is out of commission. I'm heading to my office where it's quieter." A moment later, Heather heard the click of a door and

Marco's swarthy features filled his square. "All right, I'm all yours."

"Thanks everyone. I'm glad we could pull this together on the spur of the moment," Reagan began. "I've had a bad feeling all along about that flower delivery at the reunion. We can't ignore it any longer. Somebody is threatening to kill us—they've already tried."

"We need to figure out if they have a beef with all of us or just some of us," Josh chimed in.

"I wondered about that too," Heather said. "I think they're enjoying the fact that we don't know for sure."

"What kind of a sick, twisted person does stuff like this?" Sydney exclaimed.

"If we knew that we wouldn't be on this call right now, would we?" Marco grumbled.

"I didn't organize this to waste our time bickering," Reagan said in a reproving tone.

"That's precisely what we're doing—wasting time," Marco shot back. "I have a restaurant to run."

"All right, let's calm down and try not to snip at one another," Josh interjected. "We're all upset and on edge, but it doesn't do us any good to lose our focus. We're here to work together and, with Heather's help, to get to the bottom of this. I'm going to suggest that we take our cues from her. She's the only one of us who has any experience investigating crime, so I'm guessing she has a few ideas worth listening to."

Heather gave a tight smile, grateful for Josh's ability to smooth things over, but reluctant to appear as if she was taking the reins away from an already agitated Reagan.

"All right, Heather, how should we go about this?" Reagan asked, arching a disgruntled brow. "Do we make a list of possible suspects, or what?"

"That would be a good place to start," Heather affirmed. "Think about anyone in your past or present who might have a motive to hurt you."

"Who hates us enough to try and kill us, you mean," Marco cut in. "Let's call it what it is. They tried to burn down my restaurant."

"Yes, but it was during the night," Sydney pointed out. "I think they were trying to send you a message, not kill you."

"You think, do you?" Marco growled. "What if they set fire to my house next, while my wife and kids are sleeping?"

"He's right," Reagan said. "What if Lucy had been hurt when I got cut off on the freeway? Our families are in danger too."

"Regardless of this person's motivation, the process remains the same," Heather said. "Make a list of anyone you can think of who might have a vested interest in hurting you."

"The obvious person who comes to mind is Roy," Reagan said. "He has a motive. And he's threatened me in the past."

Heather nodded. "Roy's a valid lead. Don't stop there though—you can't assume it's him. What about the rest of you?"

Marco scrubbed a hand over his jaw. "I can check my records and make a list of any employees I fired, although, like I said, only one of them was ticked off enough to sue me." He hesitated, frowning. "Does this mean you're coming back to Iowa? My offer to compensate you for your services still stands. Anna and I can put you up in our guest cottage for as long as it takes to work out who's behind this."

Heather blinked, momentarily caught off guard. Every face on the screen stared back at her, waiting on her response. A plethora of excuses floated to mind—she had just been to Iowa three weeks earlier, she was committed to clients in LA, she hated leaving Phoebe with the dog sitting service. Inadequate arguments in the face of what was happening. The truth was, she had to figure this out, and fast. Of the five of them, she was the best qualified. She knew where to start, what to do, how to follow up on leads, how to procure information—even how to work with the police if it came to that.

She took a deep breath, resigning herself to the only feasible course of action. If someone had found out her secret, she had to track them down and silence them.

9

For the second time in the space of a few short weeks, Heather found herself walking through the Quad Cities airport. The shock and grief she'd been experiencing when Reagan had picked her up the first time had been replaced by a sense of molten dread in the pit of her stomach. She couldn't shake the feeling that the messages were aimed at her, that someone was letting her know they knew the grisly secret she'd been hiding for the past two decades. She had to find out who this person was and stop them before another one of her friends ended up dead. How she would go about accomplishing that would depend a lot on who the person was and what they wanted from her. First, she needed to find them.

Her heart gave a tiny jolt when she spotted Josh striding across the terminal toward her. He was not the person she'd expected to see, but a pleasant surprise, nonetheless. She quickly arranged her expression to neutral. The last thing she needed was to complicate the situation by developing a romantic attachment. "Hey, you!" she said, hugging him in greeting. "I was expecting Reagan to pick me up."

"Yeah, I know. I took the day off work for a dental appointment, so I told her I'd swing by and get you on my way back—save her a trip. I thought maybe we could grab a coffee or something before we meet up with the others for dinner." His gaze skirted around the terminal as if searching for somewhere to settle.

A sixth sense told Heather he was uneasy about something. His ordinarily laid-back manner was muted, and he had an air of disquiet about him. He had made a concerted effort to speak to her alone, but she suspected it would be more along the lines of a professional consultation, and not a romantic overture.

"Sure, sounds great," she replied, as they headed out to the parking lot together. The grim sky overhead threatened rain. She shivered in the crisp fall breeze. LA had been basking in ninety-degree weather when she left, so it would take her a few days to adapt to the cooler temperatures in Iowa.

"Let's go to Grinders," Josh said as he turned the key in the ignition. "It's a cool new coffee house with a great vibe— all organic, Fair Trade products. Admittedly, I'm a coffee connoisseur."

"I'm more of a drive-thru coffee kind of gal myself," Heather confessed. "I'm always darting off to a job, and even if I have time to kill, I don't like sitting at a table alone."

"I thought you'd be used to it by now," Josh responded, his gaze brushing over her.

She felt her cheeks flush. "I don't eat out very often. It's easier to pick something up and take it home."

Josh gave a knowing nod. "I get it. The not-so-discreet eyebrow raise when you ask for a table for one, not to mention the pitying smile of the waiter when he removes a place setting."

Seated in a booth at the back of the cafe, Heather wrapped her fingers around her caramel cappuccino, inhaling the rich, nutty scent, and looked expectantly across at Josh. "I appreciate you picking me up at the airport, but I get the feeling we're not just here to socialize."

He gave her an abashed grin. "I'm not going to deny it. I had to talk to you, alone."

Heather's stomach did a subtle flip. For a second, her concentration slipped, and her eyes glazed over as she imagined Josh confessing his attraction to her, that he'd brought her here because—"

"Heather? Are you listening?"

"Yes! Sorry! Go ahead." Blinking, she took a hasty gulp of her cappuccino, scorching her lips in the process.

Josh gave a tentative chuckle. "You zoned out there for a minute."

"Just jet-lagged after the flights, I guess. So, what was it you wanted to talk to me about?"

He dropped his gaze, picking at the cardboard sleeve on his coffee cup. "I haven't said anything to the others—it's a bit of a delicate situation—but with everything that's going on, I'm worried there might be a connection. I thought I'd run it by you first."

"I'm listening," Heather prompted.

"I've been thinking about what you said, to consider anyone who might have a motive to hurt us. And the fact is, there is one person who comes to mind." He dragged in a heavy breath as he leaned back in his chair. "This is difficult to talk about. I'm struggling with guilt over the whole situation."

"I'm not here to judge you," Heather assured him. She took a sip of her cappuccino and waited for him to continue.

If only he knew the truth. She was hardly in a position to judge anyone.

"I had this client a few months back," Josh said, straightening up and looking intently across at Heather. "Ruby Wilcox. She was an ex-model—a beautiful woman—but she suffered from anxiety and depression. It was affecting her marriage. Her husband was frustrated, and he didn't know how to help her." He hesitated, raising his brows a fraction. "I'm sure you can guess where this is going already."

"Talk me through it," Heather urged, quashing the pinprick of jealousy that had stirred at the thought of Josh and an ex-model sharing intimate conversations—and possibly more—in his office.

"After a couple of months of therapy, she began to latch onto me. It happens occasionally. It's called transference when a patient attaches affection to their doctor." He took a small sip of his coffee before continuing. "As a professional, I understood exactly what was happening. She viewed me as her lifeboat. As a lonely man who'd been divorced a little over a year, I admit some part of me enjoyed the attention. Nothing happened between us, of course—I'm not that unethical. But, after one of her sessions, she went home and told her husband she was in love with me and wanted a divorce. Naturally, it didn't go over well. He showed up in my office the next day threatening to kill me if I didn't leave his wife alone. I didn't report it to the police at the time, because I felt guilty for not taking action earlier. I referred her to another one of my colleagues after that."

Heather gave a small shrug. "You did all you could have done under the circumstances. Was that the end of it?"

Josh grimaced. "I wish." He exhaled a heavy breath and rubbed his forehead. "She committed suicide two days later."

Heather fought to keep her shock under wraps. "Did she leave a suicide note?"

"No, thankfully. If she'd even hinted about having feelings for me, I might have been hauled in front of the ethics board—lost my license even."

"So now you're wondering if her husband is behind what's been going on?"

"I realize it's unlikely. Especially as it was Marco's restaurant that was targeted, not my practice." Josh paused and scratched his jaw. "But I wondered if he might have seen me hanging out there with Marco and thought I was one of the owners or something. At any rate, I wanted to run it by you and get your take."

Heather removed the plastic lid from her cappuccino and took another sip, licking the foam from her upper lip before responding. "Text me the details and I'll do a little investigating on the side. It's an angle worth pursuing, if only for the purpose of elimination. If you do decide to tell the others, just tell them you had a patient who committed suicide and her husband blamed you—leave out the part about her being attracted to you." Heather arched a meaningful brow at him. "You don't want any rumors starting to circulate that could negatively impact your practice."

"You mean ... Reagan?" He flattened his lips into a tight line. "Say no more, I get it. Look, thanks for helping me out with this. To be honest, I didn't know how you'd feel about me after hearing what I had to say."

"Why would I feel any differently about you? You're only human, like the rest of us." Heather gave a laugh that sounded hollow even to her own ears. What Josh had done was understandable, and forgivable—he'd been hurting and lonely after his divorce. On the other hand, *you're only human* was not an adequate excuse for what she had done.

Her heart had been hard as steel that night—the guilt had come much later.

"We should get going," Josh said, glancing at his watch. "Traffic will be heavy getting across town at this time of day. Are you staying with your sister this trip?"

"Violet's in Boston—she gets back tomorrow. I'm bunking at Marco's guest cottage tonight. I might stay with Violet after that. It all depends what her plans are and how long I'm here. I don't want to wear out my welcome."

"I doubt you could do that," Josh said, gathering up their paper cups and napkins.

Heather threw him a curious glance as she got to her feet, trying to decide if he was talking about Violet, or Marco, or himself.

At The Sardinian, Marco's flagship restaurant on the far side of town, Josh and Heather joined the others in a private room at the back. After they were seated, Marco gestured to one of his wait staff hovering in the background who hurried off and returned, moments later, with a couple of bottles of wine.

"None for me, thanks," Heather said, holding her hand over her glass when the waiter approached her. "Just a Pellegrino, please."

Reagan leaned over and squeezed her arm. "We appreciate you coming back out here to investigate this."

Heather gave a tight-lipped smile. "Well, as you pointed out, I'm in it as deep as the rest of you. I take it nothing else has happened since we last spoke?"

"Not that I know of," Reagan replied, glancing around the table.

Sydney shook her head.

"I've been keeping a close eye on the restaurants, making sure no one suspicious is loitering in the vicinity, and I've installed some additional cameras. Nothing out of the ordinary to report," Marco said.

"Nothing on my end either," Josh added. He met Heather's gaze briefly before looking away.

The waiter interrupted them to take their orders. As soon as he retreated, Reagan set a yellow legal pad on the table and retrieved a pen from her purse. "Let's get right to business. I've begun making a list of suspects for Heather to follow up on. So far, it's just my ex—Roy—and a nosy old retired neighbor who makes a habit of calling the city to complain about where Dave leaves the trashcan, that kind of thing."

Marco let out a humph of disgust. He swirled his wine around in his glass before taking a swig. "A grouchy pensioner hardly fits the profile of an arsonist. We're not here to waste Heather's time."

Reagan threw him a sharp look. "I think it's important to cover all our bases. It's up to Heather to decide which leads are worth pursuing and which aren't."

Marco curled his lip and gestured for the legal pad. "I'll add Danny Baxter's contact details—the employee who sued me." He consulted his phone and scribbled something down before passing the legal pad and pen to Sydney who was sitting next to him.

She pursed her lips. "I can't think of anyone who would want to do something like this. I mean the only name I came up with is Karen Hill—Steve's ex-fiancée. He broke off his engagement to her to be with me, which sucked, I admit, but that was fifteen years ago. I doubt she's still resentful about it after all this time."

"Add her name to the list anyway," Reagan insisted, jabbing a finger at the legal pad.

Sydney shrugged and picked up the pen. "I don't have

any current contact information for her—just her maiden name. She lived in Moline."

"That's all I need," Heather said. "I can take it from there."

Sydney made a note of it and then handed the pad to Heather. "How about you? I'm sure you have all sorts of unsavory characters out for your blood in LA," she said, with a look of mock horror.

Heather shrugged. "Pretty much every case I work on. There's always big money involved. So, yes, I'm a potential target. But if someone wanted to do a hit job on me, it would be a lot easier to pull off in LA than following me out to Iowa." She passed the legal pad to Josh. "You're next. Do you have anyone to add?"

He rubbed his jaw, an uneasy expression on his face. "I … had this patient who committed suicide a few months back. Her husband blamed me for not being able to help her. He came into my office and threatened to kill me. I never saw him again after that, so I didn't report it to the police." He jotted something down on the pad and handed it back to Heather.

"So what's the next step?" Reagan asked, a curious gleam in her eye.

"First, I'm going to prioritize the names on this list," Heather said, glancing it over. "I'll do some research, run some background checks, and then determine who is worth pursuing. If anyone else comes to mind in the meantime, text me the information. Also, think back to the reunion. Did you notice anyone acting suspiciously that night? Reagan, maybe you can get me a list of everyone who volunteered on the reunion committee. We can't rule out the possibility that the person was working alongside you."

Reagan shot a wary look in Marco's direction. "Well,

there was Marco, Josh, Sydney, and myself, obviously. Lindsay too, until the accident. There were ten of us altogether. I'll print you out a list."

"Speaking of the reunion," Sydney interjected, "Did you find out anything more about the floral delivery?"

Heather shook her head. "All we know is that the customer paid in cash—a woman. No camera on the premises and the description was vague. She could have been hired by someone to place the order."

"I did a little research on the significance of the forget-me-not flower and how it got its name," Sydney said. "Supposedly, two lovers walking along the Danube River spotted the flowers on a bank. They thought they were unusual looking so the man climbed down to pick some and ended up falling in. As he was being swept away to his death, he yelled out to the woman not to forget him. So she named the flowers after him. *Forget-me-not.* Kind of creepy, huh?"

An uncomfortable silence fell over the table. Everyone stopped eating and stared at Sydney.

Heather's blood ran cold. It felt as if a voice from beyond the grave had just called to her.

10

Alone in Marco's guest cottage later that evening, Heather threw herself down on the bed and stared up at the wood-beamed ceiling. Sydney's words haunted her like a ghostly rebuke from her past. *Forget ... me ... not!* All she'd tried to do for the past two decades was forget: forget what happened to Violet and—more important—forget what she'd done about it afterward. But some things couldn't be forgotten no matter how much time trickled by. It had all begun with a lie. A relatively harmless lie, or so she'd thought at the time.

"This kid in my class is having a party for all the freshmen," Violet had chirped as they drove home from school at the end of the first week of term. "Sort of an icebreaker. You know Mom and Dad won't let me go if I ask them. But all my friends are going. Can you tell them you're taking me to the movies or something and drop me off at the party?"

Heather tightened her grip on the steering wheel and

glanced over at Violet with a raised brow. "Don't tell me you've got your eye on some boy already."

Violet tossed her head. "Of course not. It's just that everyone else is going and I hate being the only one who's never allowed to do anything fun."

"So who is this kid and where does he live?" Heather asked. At seventeen, she had been fiercely protective of her vivacious fourteen-year-old sister, but at the same time, she knew better than anyone how unbearably strict their father could be. Heather's curfew had been 9:00 p.m. until she was sixteen, which meant she'd missed out on many a fun activity with her friends. The one time she'd invited them over to watch a movie at her house had been a disaster. Her father had insisted on watching it with them and fast forwarded through the PG-rated kissing scene. Thanks to their mother's coaxing on their behalf, he'd eased up a little since then, and now that she was a senior, he'd agreed to let her and Violet stay out until 11:30 p.m. on the weekend as long as they were together and took their mother's new flip phone with them.

"The kid who's throwing the party is Trevor Carpenter," Violet said. "His parents own a sandwich shop in Davenport. They're very respectable. I have the address. We can drive by their house if you want to check it out."

"Let me think about it," Heather replied, cranking up the music in the car.

In the end, against her better judgment, she had agreed to pretend she was taking Violet to the movies on the night of the party and promised their parents to bring her straight home afterward. After dropping Violet off at the Carpenters' house, Heather sat in the car and watched for a few minutes as freshmen arrived in pairs and small groups, talking and laughing excitedly. She was relieved to see there weren't any older kids showing up. She glanced at her watch. It was a little after eight. She was reluctant to go to the movies in case Violet decided she wanted to leave early. On the other hand, she might want to stay until the party ended, which would leave Heather with three hours to kill. She didn't dare risk going to any of her friends' houses in case it got back to her parents. She might as well catch a movie.

Two hours later, Heather was melded to her seat, lost in the plot of a compelling drama when her phone rang, startling her almost out of her skin.

She quickly got to her feet and exited the theater, pressing the phone to her ear to drown out the chatter of the other patrons lining up for popcorn in the foyer. "I can't hear what you're saying," Heather said. "Slow down. I'm on my way to pick you up."

"Please hurry, Heather!" Violet sobbed into the phone.

"Why? What's wrong? Did something happen?" She broke into a jog, ignoring the reproving looks hurled her way as she dashed through the double doors and out to the parking lot.

"Just hurry up and get here," Violet begged, before dissolving into tears once more.

"I'm getting in my car right now," Heather assured her before peeling out of the parking lot. "Listen to me, Violet. I'll be there in ten minutes. Don't hang up. Now, tell me what happened. Are you hurt? Is someone else hurt?"

"I'm ... I'm ..." Violet sniffed a few times and then whispered, "I can't talk now. There are kids here waiting to be picked up. I'll meet you outside at the curb."

"It isn't safe, Violet. Wait inside. I'll come to the door when I get there."

"There's a bunch of other people outside too. I'll be fine."

"Just promise me you won't stay out there by yourself," Heather said, trying to curb her exasperation. "Are Trevor's parents there?"

"They went next door to have a drink with their neighbors."

"Then go next door and wait with them."

"No! I ... I can't do that."

Heather's stomach churned. Violet's voice sounded desperate. But at least she wasn't hurt. Maybe she'd had a falling out with her friends, or someone had said something mean to her. Whatever it was, Heather needed to get there fast. Her sister was upset, and it pained her to listen to her crying into the phone.

Minutes later, Heather pulled into the cul-de-sac where she'd dropped Violet off. Several clusters of kids were milling around outside the house chatting and laughing. Violet sat alone on a small retaining wall, hunched over and staring at the ground. At the sound of the car approaching, she glanced up and immediately vaulted to her feet and ran to meet it. Once inside, she sank down in the passenger seat and hugged her arms to herself.

"Violet! Are you all right?" Heather asked, tamping down the note of alarm in her voice. "What on earth is going on with you?"

"Nothing. Please take me home."

"Did you have a falling out with your friends or something?"

Violet stared straight ahead. "Please, just drive."

Heather gave an irritated shrug. "Put your seatbelt on." She turned the car around and pulled out of the subdivision and onto the main road, mulling over how best to handle the situation. They had a fifteen-mile drive ahead of them. But would it be enough time to tease whatever was bothering Violet out of her? She would have to drive slowly and take the long way home. She couldn't take Violet back to the house in this state or their parents would launch a full-blown interrogation.

"Violet, will you please talk to me?" Heather prodded, after a couple of miles of silence had stretched between them. "Mom and Dad are going to ask a million questions if you arrive back in this state."

Violet tilted her face toward her, her tear-filled eyes widening in horror. "No! You can't let them. Tell them I'm really tired and I want to go to bed."

"I'm not going to lie to them again tonight unless you tell me what's going on," Heather responded, raising her voice. "I'm the one who took you to that party and if something happened, I need to know about it. I'm responsible."

Violet's lip began to tremble. "It's not your fault. It's ... mine. I was ... I was drinking."

"What?" Heather couldn't keep the shock out of her voice. She gritted her teeth, fighting the urge to pull over and shake her sister. "How could you be so stupid? And where did you get the alcohol from anyway?"

"Some kids brought vodka in water bottles," Violet whimpered.

Heather's thoughts were racing as she tried to figure out what kind of damage control she would have to do. It was bad, but it could have been worse. At least she hadn't thrown up all over herself. She just had to get Violet into the house, past her parents and straight to bed without engaging them in conversation. If they saw the state she was in, they would know immediately something was wrong. Violet was sure to break down and confess that she'd been drinking. And then they'd both be grounded for the rest of the year. Heather was not about to let that happen her senior year. "I can't believe you were that stupid, Violet. We talked about this."

"I know, I know," she sobbed, rocking back and forth in her seat.

Heather sighed. "Look, I'm sorry for yelling. Calm down. This is my fault for agreeing to lie for you in the first place. Here's what we'll do. When we get to the house, I'll say you need the bathroom. Run straight upstairs. Don't come back down. And for goodness sake, clean your teeth. Pretend to be asleep if Mom or Dad check on you. Got it?"

Violet nodded mutely and curled up on her side, staring out the side window. They rode in silence for the rest of the way home, pulling up at their house a little after 11:30 p.m.

The porch light came on and their mother appeared at the front door. "Thank goodness you're home," she called to them as they exited the car. "Your father was about to head into town to look for you."

"Don't be silly," Heather called back. "I told you the movie wasn't over until eleven."

Her mother flapped a hand at her. "You know how your father worries."

"Don't forget, straight to bed," Heather muttered to Violet, as soon as their mother disappeared back inside. "I'll handle Mom and Dad."

Violet gave a tentative nod and followed Heather to the front door. She made a beeline for the stairs while Heather walked back to the kitchen where her mother and father were seated at the table clutching mugs of chamomile tea.

Her mother smiled up at her. "Well, how was—?"

"Where's your sister?" Her father cut in, jerking his chin sideways—a nervous habit he'd had as far back as Heather could remember.

"Bathroom." Heather gave a wry grin. "She's been trying to hold it the whole way home."

"Did you girls enjoy the movie?" her mother asked.

"Yeah, it was great," Heather replied, diving into a lengthy synopsis of the plot designed to buy Violet enough time to clean her teeth and get into bed.

When she'd finished, her father got to his feet. "I'm going to check on your sister." He came back downstairs a few minutes later and resumed his seat at the table. "She's fast asleep." He scratched the back of his neck. "I still think she's far too young to be going to the late movie."

His wife laid a hand on his arm. "Honey, it's the weekend, she'll be fine. She can sleep in tomorrow."

"I'm going to head to bed too," Heather said, stifling an exaggerated yawn. She kissed both her parents on the cheek and then made her way upstairs to the room she shared with Violet. After closing the door quietly behind her, she whispered, "Vivi, are you awake?"

Violet sat up in bed and drew her knees to her chest.

Heather plonked down next to her and wrapped an arm around her shoulders. "You can stop worrying now. It's all right. They didn't suspect a thing."

A guttural sob racked Violet's tiny frame.

Heather pulled her closer and rocked her gently back-and-forth. "It's okay. You learned your lesson. Put it behind you now."

Violet pulled away and pressed the backs of her hands to her eyes. "You don't understand. I can't."

"Now you're just being dramatic," Heather said. "You're not the only teenager who's taken a drink and regretted it. It's over and done with. Forget about it."

Violet blinked at her, her pale face glistening with tears. "I don't mean the vodka. I mean the rape."

11

Neither Heather nor Violet had slept much that night. Instead, they held each other and cried for hours on end. Heather tried to persuade Violet that they needed to tell their parents what had happened. But Violet resisted with every fiber in her being, insisting she didn't know who the kid was or even his real name—only that he was older and that he'd gone by *Tank*. He had arrived at the party with a friend an hour or so after Heather dropped Violet off. She had flirted with him in the kitchen and let him kiss her—the vodka lowering her inhibitions. Later on that evening, he'd followed her into a bathroom, locked the door behind him, and threatened to strangle her if she screamed.

"I don't want the kids in school to know what happened," Violet choked out. "If we tell Dad everyone will hear about it. He'll want to press charges, go to the media even. He'll never let me out of the house again. My life will be over."

In the end, Heather had agreed to say nothing, fearing her father might do something drastic if the police managed to identify Tank. She had settled for making Violet take multiple pregnancy tests over the ensuing weeks—all of which came back negative. Her parents noticed a change in Violet's ordinarily bubbly demeanor, but Heather convinced them it was merely hormones.

Two months later, Heather was pulling into a gas station after a day out shopping with her sister in Davenport when Violet gripped her by the arm. "Wait!" she hissed in an urgent whisper.

"Ouch! What are you doing?" Heather said, throwing a befuddled glance at Violet who had slithered down several inches in the passenger seat.

"It's him," she whispered. "Tank—the guy who raped me!"

Every nerve in Heather's body began to pulse in unison. "Where?" she demanded.

"Filling up that old green truck at pump number seven, the guy with his back to us. I saw his face when we were pull—"

Before Violet could finish, Heather was out of the car. "Hey!" she yelled, to the six-foot-two, broad-shouldered male in a Hawkeyes ball cap who was unscrewing the gas cap on his truck.

His eyes narrowed momentarily and then flicked to the car where Violet was staring at him through the windscreen. His body tensed. In a flash, he jumped back in his truck and took off, gas cap dangling.

Heather inhaled a quick breath to calm her racing heart before dashing back to her car. She climbed in and gripped the steering wheel tightly, her knuckles whitening under the pressure. "We'll never catch him now. The light just changed. Did you get a picture?"

Violet gave a defeated shake of her head. "No. I ... didn't think to take one." Her eyes filled with tears. "I froze."

"It's all right," Heather assured her. "I know what he looks like now." She got back out of her car to gas up, already assembling a game plan in her head. She would make it her business to find Tank, no matter how long it took, and when she did, she would make him pay for what he'd done to Violet.

In the following weeks, she'd trawled private investigator websites, researching how to track down people and learning ways to stalk them. Looking back, it had been her first real case—hunting for Violet's attacker. The case that had launched her career.

Unbeknownst to her parents, she spent all her spare time staked out close to the gas station. She figured Tank must live or work close by, and she was banking on him returning at some point. No one at school had any idea what she was up to. Lindsay was the one person she trusted with her deepest secrets, but she hesitated even to tell her, until the day Lindsay spilled her guts about a secret of her own. "I need to tell you something, but first you have to swear you won't tell a soul."

Heather reached for the Jelly Belly bag on the floor next to her. "Okay."

Lindsay giggled nervously. "Don't freak out, but I've been seeing my boss."

"Are you serious?" Heather exclaimed, picturing the car wash where Lindsay worked on the weekends. "That guy with the ponytail?"

"I'm not talking about my immediate boss," Lindsay said coyly, "I mean the owner."

Heather's jaw dropped. "How old is he?"

Lindsay gave a nonchalant shrug. "Thirty-eight. I don't

care about his age so don't give me any grief. We're in love and that's all that matters. He's going to leave his wife once I graduate. Until then, he doesn't want me telling anyone about us."

"But he's more than twice your age," Heather protested.

"So? Boys our age are idiots. Bill knows where he's going in life. He's traveled all over the world, he went to—"

"But he's married!" Heather cut in. "Does he have kids?"

"Twins, but they're older—sophomores in college."

"You're still breaking up a family," Heather pointed out. "Remember how you felt when your dad left?"

"Bill and his wife grew apart before he met me. I'm not breaking anything up that wasn't already broken," Lindsay huffed.

"That's what he's telling you," Heather said. "You're younger than his kids, for crying out loud. I bet his wife might have something to say about it. And what about his business? If he divorces her, he might have to sell it. You could end up destroying their livelihood."

"He's going to buy her out." Lindsay grinned at Heather and shook her playfully. "Don't be such a worrywart. Trust me, Bill's got everything worked out. We're not doing anything illegal. I'm eighteen in a few weeks, remember? Speaking of which, what are you doing for your eighteenth? A party?"

Heather shrugged. "I don't know."

Lindsay arched a brow at her. "You sound like you don't even care."

"I don't anymore." Heather's voice cracked. "Look, there's something I need to tell you too, but you can't tell anyone, ever."

Lindsay widened her eyes. "Are you seeing someone as well? Your dad's going to kill you when he finds—"

"No! That's not it!" Heather snapped. She dropped her head into her hands. "I wish that's all it was. It's so much worse."

Lindsay draped an arm around her shoulder. "I'm sorry. I was caught up in my own excitement. I know something's been bothering you lately. You've been so quiet. Is it because of the rumors at school? Don't worry, if Reagan's behind it, it will all come out in the end. You know I'll support you. We've always been there for each other."

"It's not that." Heather pulled anxiously at her lip. "Remember the party Violet went to—the one my parents didn't know about?"

"Oh no! Don't tell me they found out!"

"No. But something happened at the party."

Lindsay's jaw dropped. "Did Violet get busted drinking?"

"She was drinking," Heather admitted. "Some kids brought vodka in their water bottles. She knew better, but she didn't want to be the only one left out, so she had a few shots. Then some older kids showed up later that evening. Violet was tipsy by then and she was flirting with one of them. A big kid—he called himself Tank."

Lindsay grimaced. "That's not good if it gets back to your dad."

"It gets worse. He followed her into a bathroom and ... and he raped her."

Lindsay clapped a hand over her mouth and stared at Heather, eyes bulging in horror. When she spoke, her voice was a subdued whisper. "Did you report it?"

Heather shook her head. "I wanted to, but Violet begged me not to. She doesn't even know the kid's real name. She's mortified at the thought of everyone at school finding out. And of course, Dad would never let either of us out of the house again if he found out."

"But it's a crime," Lindsay cried. "You can't let him get away with it."

Heather pinned a penetrating look on her. "I'm not going to let him get away with it. I know what he looks like now, and what kind of truck he drives. Violet spotted him at a gas station a couple of weeks back and pointed him out to me. He looks like a football player. He's not from our high school. I'm guessing he's at least nineteen or twenty. I've been staking out the gas station ever since. If he comes back, I'm going to follow him and find out where he lives."

Lindsay fussed nervously with her ponytail. "That sounds dangerous. What if he tries to run you off the road or something?"

"He won't. I'll be discreet about it."

"So what's the point of following him to his house then?"

Heather pulled her brows together in concentration. "I'm not sure yet. I need to confront him about what he did —it all depends how he reacts, I suppose."

"You can't confront him. It's not like he's going to beg for forgiveness. He might hurt you too."

Heather locked eyes with Lindsay. "I put one of my dad's shotguns in my car, just in case I need to scare him off. Don't worry, I won't use it."

Lindsay jumped up and began pacing back and forth. "I don't like the sound of this. It could go horribly wrong. You should either go to the police and report him or forget all about him."

"I can't break Violet's trust!" Heather blurted out. "My hands are tied. I just need to make him realize what he's done. If he's remorseful, maybe I can move on."

"What do you mean *you* can move on? You weren't the one he raped."

"It was my fault it happened," Heather said. "I shouldn't

have lied to our parents or taken Violet to the stupid party in the first place. I owe it to her to make him acknowledge what he's done."

Lindsay set her lips in a grim line. "Promise me you won't confront him alone. I'll go with you."

Heather shook her head. "I have to go after him the minute I spot him—I might have only one shot."

As it turned out, it was several months later before Heather's chance came. She was sitting in her car doing her math homework one Saturday evening shortly before 10:00 p.m. when the green truck pulled into the gas station.

Her heart thumped like galloping hooves against her ribs as she slowly slid up in her seat. She watched Tank climb out of his truck and fish a credit card from his back pocket. It was him all right. And he was alone. Her persistence had been rewarded. She peered over her shoulder at the blanket on the back seat covering her dad's shotgun. She had told Lindsay she was only bringing it along as a deterrent, but she'd use it if she had to. Her father had taken her and Violet hunting from a young age, and she wasn't afraid to pull the trigger.

Once the green truck pulled out onto the road, Heather turned her key in the ignition and followed at a safe distance. Tank had the driver's window rolled down and was resting his elbow casually on the frame. Heavy metal music pounded into the night as they left town and headed into corn country. The truck swerved once or twice before correcting course, leading Heather to suspect he'd been drinking. She slowed down, increasing the distance between them, and let the truck disappear from sight. They were the only two vehicles on the road and she didn't want to make it obvious to Tank that he had someone on his tail. She drove at a steady speed for the next couple of miles, occasionally spotting the truck's taillights as it rounded a bend or shot through a junction. She wasn't familiar with the area, but she estimated they were ten or fifteen miles out of town.

Turning a corner, she abruptly slammed on the brakes. Tank's truck was parked at an angle across the road, blocking her route. She put her car in park and sat frozen in her seat, scarcely breathing, her eyes scouring the darkness for any sign of movement. Moments later, the truck door swung open. Tank staggered out and began walking unsteadily toward her. Instinctively, she reached behind her for the shotgun.

He stumbled up to her car and slammed both palms on the driver's window startling her out of her skin. "Why're you following me?" he yelled, slurring his words as he beat his fist on the roof for emphasis. Heather sat as still as possible, the gun resting across her knees. He was drunk, which meant his reactions would be unpredictable. There was no sense in rolling down her window and trying to engage him in conversation.

All of a sudden, he stepped back and swung a vicious kick at her door. "Open the door! *Now!*"

Heather scooted toward the center console, and then slowly raised the shotgun and pressed the muzzle to the window.

Tank lowered his face to the glass, a confused expression flitting across his features before his eyes widened. For a moment he hesitated, as if debating with himself, before turning and stumbling back to his truck. He climbed in, revved the engine, and tore off down the road, leaving a cloud of dust in his wake. Heather let out a long sigh of relief as she returned the gun to the rear seat. Mustering her resolve, she floored the gas pedal, and gave chase. Her pulse pounded in her temples as she careened around corners at a speed she'd never driven at before. Adrenalin flooded her system. She wasn't sure what she was going to do when she caught up with Tank again, but she knew one thing—she wasn't going to let him disappear. She accelerated, trying desperately to keep the truck's taillights in view. She couldn't allow him to get far enough ahead to pull off in some corn field and turn off his lights, while she roared obliviously past him. As she approached another bend in the road, the screech of tires reached her ears, followed by an eerie crunching sound. She slammed on the brakes as she wheeled around the corner, coming to a sudden halt at the sight of the green truck folded around a tree. Shaking, she pulled over to the side of the road.

For several minutes she stayed put in her vehicle, fearing the truck door would burst open and Tank would tumble out, more enraged than ever. When he failed to emerge, she gingerly opened her door and climbed out. She stood in the darkness next to her car agonizing over what to do before finally reaching into the back seat and grabbing the shotgun. She couldn't take anything for granted. He might be waiting for her—ready to pounce the minute she let down her guard.

Cautiously, she approached the truck, taking aim at the driver's window. Her heart skipped a beat when she glimpsed Tank slumped over the steering wheel, blood dripping down the side of his head. Her chest rose and fell as her breath came in shallow spurts. She had set out tonight to hold him accountable for what he had done. It seemed fate had intervened on her behalf and dealt the fatal blow.

She pulled a shaky breath together as she lowered the shotgun and stared into the cab. A crushed beer can lay amid the debris on the passenger seat. A part of her wanted to open the door and root around for his ID—find out the real name of the scumbag who'd so callously stolen Violet's innocence. A shiver crossed her shoulders. She couldn't do it. The thought of touching him, maybe even getting his blood on her hands was utterly repulsive. She backed away a few steps and then froze. Had he just twitched? Or had she imagined it? For a long moment, she remained rooted to the spot watching in morbid fascination, willing him to be dead. A beat later, he lifted his head like a wobbly newborn and looked around, his eyes coming to rest on her. Slowly, he slid a bloodied palm up the inside of the glass. It looked like he was mouthing: *Help!*

A finger of dread worked its way over Heather's shoulders. He wasn't dead, after all. He was clinging to life and asking for mercy—mercy he hadn't shown Violet. Heather hesitated, the overriding desire for revenge clawing at her insides, insisting on having its way. She clenched a fist at her side, sealing in her decision before walking resolutely back to her car. She rammed it into gear and turned around in the road, before heading back the way she had come.

She wasn't going to save the man who had raped her sister. There would be no 911 call.

12

Back at her house that night, Heather tossed and turned in her bed, drenched with sweat. Each time she began to drift off, she would jerk awake at the haunting image of Tank's bloodshot eyes latching onto hers, fingers pressed to the glass of the driver's window in a desperate plea for help. Curled up in a ball beneath her duvet, she listened to the sound of Violet breathing, wondering if Tank had already taken his last breath, trapped in his truck. In the eyes of the law, she was a murderer. Granted, she hadn't used the shotgun. But she'd fled the scene of an accident. She had knowingly and willingly left another human being to die.

She desperately needed to talk to Lindsay—Lindsay would be there for her no matter what, just like Heather had been there for Lindsay when her relationship with her boss had come to an abrupt end a few weeks prior. Bill's wife had found out about the affair and promptly filed for divorce, but instead of the proposal Lindsay had been eagerly anticipating, Bill had upped and disappeared without a measly goodbye, much less a forwarding address.

At six-thirty the following morning, Heather finally broke down and called Lindsay.

"I found Tank."

"What? Did you get his address?"

"I need to talk to you. Can I come over?"

"Uh, okay. I'll unlock the back door for you."

By the time Heather got to Lindsay's house, she was shaking uncontrollably, partly from lack of sleep, partly from delayed shock. Somehow in the light of day, the horror of what she had done hit harder than under the cover of darkness when she'd almost been able to convince herself it was all a bad dream.

"You look awful," Lindsay blurted out the moment she opened the door to her. She hustled Heather inside and upstairs to her room, stifling a yawn. "My mom's still asleep. She won't bother us, but I'll lock the door to be safe." She turned on some music before sinking into her enormous furry beanbag chair next to Heather. "So, what happened? Did you find out where he lived?"

Heather inhaled a steadying breath and shook her head. "He realized someone was following him. We were about fifteen miles or so west of town. When I came around a corner, he had blocked the road with his truck."

Lindsay let out a strangled gasp. "I warned you not to go after him on your own. What happened then?"

"He started yelling at me. He was punching my car the whole time and kicking it. He'd been drinking."

"He didn't hurt you, did he?" Lindsay asked, her eyes alight with concern.

"No. I held the shotgun up to the window and scared him off. I think he realized then who I was—he saw me that day at the gas station with Violet."

"So you lost him?"

"I let him get just far enough ahead of me so that I could still see his taillights in the distance. He was driving erratically, way too fast. And then ..."

"Then what?" Lindsay prodded, her voice wavering.

"He crashed into a tree."

Lindsay pulled her brows together. "Is he ... injured?"

Heather blinked back tears, bile seeping up her throat. "I waited in my car for a minute or two, but he didn't get out, so I went over to check on him. I took the shotgun, in case it was a trap. It was horrible. His head was flopped forward, there was blood everywhere." She gulped back a sob. "I was about to head back to my car when I saw him twitch. At first, I thought I'd imagined it. But then he lifted his head and looked straight at me."

Lindsay's gaze was riveted on her, horror pooling in her eyes. "Did you call 911?"

"No," Heather choked out the word. "I ... I drove away."

"Seriously? You left him there? We have to call someone —the police."

"We can't!" Heather gripped Lindsay's sleeve. "I can't tell them I was following him. How would I explain that? Tank might say I threatened him with a gun. I could be held responsible for the crash."

"No you won't. He was drinking and driving. I'll call the police for you, if you want."

"Then you'd have to tell them how you know about the crash. They'll want to question me." Heather groaned and dropped her head into her hands.

Lindsay frowned. "I could call it in anonymously. That's what you should have done last night."

Heather let out a sob. "I know, I know. You don't always make the best decisions either."

"It's okay," Lindsay soothed. "I'm not trying to beat you up about it. You were in shock. You weren't thinking straight."

Heather smoothed her hair back from her tear-streaked face. "That's not exactly true. I knew what I was doing when I drove off. I told myself if it wasn't meant to be, someone would find him. And if he died, then justice would be served for what he did to Violet."

Lindsay gave a wary nod. "All right, so what do you want to do now? We could drive out there and see if ... you know, if he's still—"

"No!" Heather gave a firm shake of her head. "Someone's bound to have found him by now. Emergency crews might be there. And cops hanging around asking questions. We might look suspicious—we don't live on that road and we don't have any business being out there. Let's wait and see if there's anything about it on the local news this morning."

Lindsay frowned. "I mean, he's probably not dead. Maybe it wasn't as serious as you thought. He might have got out and walked home for all you know. Serves him right if his truck is totaled."

"I don't think he was up to walking anywhere." Heather closed her eyes and let out a long, shuddering sigh. "I'm not saying I want him dead, but I sort of hope he is, if that makes any sense."

Lindsay ran her fingers through her ponytail. "I get it. But I still think you should have called 911." She uncurled her legs and got to her feet. "Want some breakfast? We can talk about what to do afterward."

"No thanks," Heather said, the thought of food sending waves of nausea through her belly.

"You will once you smell my blueberry pancakes. I'll

make us some hot chocolate too. You could use the sugar. You're still shaking like a leaf."

Lindsay was in the process of pouring the pancakes onto the griddle when her mother walked into the kitchen, belting her robe around her waist. "Heather! How are you, Sweetie?"

"Hi, Mrs. Robinson," she mumbled.

"Do you want some pancakes, Mom?" Lindsay asked.

"No thanks, dear. I just need a coffee to jump start my system. You girls are up early for a Saturday. Off somewhere special this morning?" she asked, as she crossed the kitchen to the coffee maker.

"Nope," Lindsay replied as she stacked the pancakes on a plate. "Just hanging out. I've got a history assignment to do later on." She grabbed some silverware and signaled with a dramatic tilt of her head for Heather to follow her into the dining room. After placing the pancakes on the table between them, she proceeded to serve Heather a plateful topped with a generous dollop of syrup and butter. "Try and eat something," she urged her. "It'll help with the shakes."

Heather picked up her knife and fork and cut off a small piece of pancake, swilling it around in the syrup and melted butter before putting it in her mouth. She chewed absent-mindedly, staring down at a lone blueberry on her plate, wondering if she was doomed to feel this emptiness inside her for the rest of her life. She had wanted to make Tank pay for what he'd done, but she hadn't set out to kill him. In the moment, she had allowed her emotions to cloud her judgement. Even Lindsay thought she'd done the wrong thing by not calling 911. It had been undeniably heartless, but her heart had been missing ever since she'd learned what Tank had done to her little sister.

"Oh no! Not again!" Lindsay's mother exclaimed. A moment later, she shuffled into the dining room in her slippers clutching a mug of steaming coffee and frowning down at the newspaper in her hand. "This is why I don't like you girls driving home late at night, especially on the weekends. There was a wreck on five-mile road last night."

Lindsay and Heather exchanged wary glances, the food on their plates instantly forgotten.

"No one we know, I hope?" Lindsay said, the pitch of her voice betraying her.

Oblivious to her daughter's agitated state, Mrs. Robinson squinted down at the news article. "They haven't identified him yet—a male in his early twenties."

"Is he bad ... badly injured?" Heather stammered.

Mrs. Robinson made a tutting sound. "A fatality. It's a crying shame. A young lad like that in the prime of his life. His poor parents. Let's see, it says here according to the Scott County Sheriff's Office, the driver was headed westbound on five-mile road shortly before 10:30 p.m. when his truck crossed the road and slammed head-on into a tree. No other vehicles were involved—well, *that's* a mercy, at least. Officers say speed was likely a factor in the crash with autopsy and toxicology test results forthcoming. First responders arrived to find the man trapped in his vehicle. He was extricated and pronounced dead at the scene. Investigators are asking anyone with information about the crash to contact the police department." She sighed and plopped herself down at the table with the girls. "Such a tragedy. A young life snuffed out like that unnecessarily. Probably been drinking by the sound of it. I'm sure his parents preached to him often enough about the dangers of drinking and driving."

Heather dropped her gaze, her skin prickling. She knew

only too well the havoc alcohol could wreak on a life. Violet had paid a heavy price for imbibing, and now her attacker had paid the ultimate price. No one would ever suspect that anything else had killed him. And that's how it would stay as long as Lindsay kept her mouth shut.

13

Heather woke with a start. She blinked around the unfamiliar room in confusion for a moment or two before it dawned on her that she was in Marco's guest cottage. It had taken her a long time to fall asleep last night after countless hours spent wrestling with the uncomfortable memories from her past. Her chest tightened with a fresh wave of pain when she remembered that Lindsay was dead. Regret that she'd let their friendship fade over the years ate at her. Lindsay had been the only person she had ever really opened up to. The aching void inside had intensified in the weeks since her friend's death. If only she were here now so that Heather could talk to her about the disturbing messages. And so Lindsay could reassure her that her secret was safe.

Throwing aside the covers, Heather climbed out of bed and tripped her way into the bathroom to shower. She didn't have time for a pity party. She had to get to work. The first thing on her agenda today was a visit to the most obvious suspect in the arson attack—Marco's disgruntled former employee, Danny Baxter. The police had interviewed him, but they hadn't gotten back to Marco with any feedback, other than to say that he had an alibi for the night in question. But Heather wanted to conduct her own interview. She knew that alibis could be bought for the right price, and she had a good sense of when someone was lying to her—a skill she'd honed over the years as an investigator.

After getting dressed and gathering up her things, she climbed into the car Marco had loaned her and took off down the driveway, waving in passing to Anna and the children who were piling into their SUV dressed for soccer. She picked up a black coffee and an egg croissant sandwich at a drive-thru, and then plugged in Danny Baxter's address to her GPS.

Twenty minutes later, she pulled up outside a nondescript, single-family home with white siding and a chain-link fence. A lone cherry tree planted in the center of the unkempt lawn was the only nod to landscaping. Heather got out of the car and ran a practiced eye around the yard, searching for any sign of a dog. If Danny had one, it was either inside or tied up in the backyard. She opened the gate and walked briskly up to the front door. The bell didn't work, so she knocked sharply on the glass oval in the door and stood back to wait. She was on the verge of knocking again, when she heard a raspy male voice call out, "Coming! Gimme a minute."

When the door opened, she found herself staring down at an unshaven male in a wheelchair. She fought to keep her expression neutral. If this was Marco's disgruntled ex-employee, he wasn't their arsonist.

"Can I help you?" he asked, running a shifty eye unabashedly up and down her frame.

"Uh, yes," she answered, scrambling to compose herself. "I live a few blocks away and I'm knocking on doors asking if anyone's seen a suspicious man loitering in the neighborhood. My daughter has been followed twice now." She wrung her hands. "The police aren't taking it seriously, so I've taken it upon myself to go door-to-door."

The man's pinched expression took on air of helpfulness. He spun around in his wheelchair and motioned for Heather to follow him. "Come on in." He led her into a musty family room with a grubby-looking chocolate-colored couch and loveseat and gestured for her to take a seat. "Can I get you something to drink, coffee, water?"

She smiled gratefully at him. "No, thank you. I don't want to take up too much of your time. I'm trying to cover as many houses as I can, as you might imagine."

He gave a thoughtful nod. "That's scary stuff about your daughter being followed."

Heather pressed her lips together. "I'm not sure if he's just targeting her, or other young girls too. I'm Janis, by the way. Sorry, I didn't think to introduce myself properly at the door. I've been in such a fluster over this."

"No worries. I'm Danny. Nice to meet you, Janis," he replied, eying her bare ring finger.

"Have you noticed any strangers hanging around lately?" she asked. "Or strange cars cruising the neighborhood?"

Danny shook his head. "Can't say I have. And I would know. I spend most of my time at home." He slapped the side of his wheelchair. "Ever since the accident."

Heather painted on a sympathetic expression. "Do you mind if I ask what happened?"

"It was a freak accident at work three months ago. The ladder slipped out from under me. I broke my back."

"I'm so sorry. What line of work are you in, Danny?"

He gave a mirthless laugh. "What line of work have I *not* been in, you mean. I was employed as a package handler at a warehouse when the accident happened. But I've done it all, painter, truck driver, waiter—"

"Really?" Heather cut in. "I worked as a waitress for years. What restaurant were you at?"

"A few different ones. Madge's Steakhouse was the most recent." He rumpled his brow. "I worked at that Italian place on the other side of town years ago—I can't remember what it's called now."

"You mean The Sardinian?"

Danny's face brightened. "Yeah, that's the one. I hear he's opened up two more locations since. I don't get around much anymore. That new fish restaurant in Moline is supposed to be good." He hesitated, as if contemplating something. Heather had a horrible feeling he might be about to ask her out. She wasted no time glancing at her phone and jumping to her feet. "I need to go. I have to be back in time to pick up my daughter. I don't want her walking home from school alone."

Danny's face fell. He spun his wheelchair around and led her back down the hallway to the front door. "It was nice to meet you, Janis. I'll keep an eye out for that creep. If you want to give me your number, I can text you if I spot anything odd."

"That's thoughtful of you, but I'm changing my phone number, as a precaution," Heather responded. "Just give the police a call directly if you see any strangers lurking around."

She made a hasty exit and hurried around the corner to where she'd parked her car. No wonder the police told Marco his disgruntled ex-employee had an alibi. It would be next to impossible to set fire to a restaurant and make a successful getaway in a wheelchair. She could eliminate Danny Baxter as a suspect, which left her right back at the theory that Marco's restaurant had been targeted to get at someone else in their group. Reagan's ex, Roy, seemed an increasingly likely culprit. She plugged his address into her phone and settled in for the drive.

When she arrived at her destination, she parked a couple of houses down and sat in the car surveilling Roy's house for several minutes. At first glance, it didn't appear that anyone was home—no signs of life, or cars in the driveway. Still, it didn't mean to say he wasn't holed up inside drinking beer and watching TV. He'd done a lot of that over the years, if Reagan was to be believed.

Heather donned her shades, climbed out and made her way to the front door. She tried ringing the doorbell several times, and then knocked before giving up and heading back to her car. She would just have to try connecting with Roy again later.

Glancing at the clock in the car, she realized she still had several hours to kill before Violet arrived back from Boston. The Wi-Fi in Marco's guest cottage sucked, and she didn't want to bother Anna by asking her if she could work at the main house. Maybe she should hang out at Violet's place until she got back—after all, Violet had told her to make herself at home.

She picked up a turkey sandwich for lunch and drove to downtown Davenport where Violet and her husband, Boyd, lived in a charming, newly renovated historic home. Heather pulled into the circular driveway and parked, marveling at how spacious the house was in comparison to her compact luxury condo back in LA. The sprawling abode was at least five-thousand square-feet and had only cost a fraction of what she'd paid for her condo.

She walked around to the back of the house and located the planter where Violet had instructed her to look for the spare key. After opening the French doors, she stepped inside the cavernous kitchen and glanced around admiringly. Violet had outdone herself with the remodel. She had always had great taste, and now she had the budget to match. Heather set down her backpack on an upholstered chair and walked over to the double refrigerator to put her sandwich away. She ran a hand over the gleaming marble surfaces atop the white oak cabinetry, smiling to herself when she noticed the security cameras tucked away in discrete locations. She had been the one who had encouraged Violet and Boyd to install them during the remodel. Years of working as a private investigator had taught her that a small investment in home safety paid for itself in the long run.

After fishing her laptop out of her backpack, Heather headed out to the patio off the kitchen at the back of the house to enjoy some late fall sunshine while she worked. She had access to several proprietary databases that would allow her to run background checks on the list of suspects she'd been given at dinner last night. She would begin with Reagan's ex—Roy. Of all the names that had come up, he seemed to Heather to be the only one who fit the bill. He had a long history of violent behavior, and a strong motive to go after both Reagan and Marco.

Engrossed in her work, she jumped at the sound of voices. Glancing up, she caught a glimpse of Violet and Boyd through the glass.

Violet's face lit up at the sight of her. She tossed the mail in her hand on the kitchen table and then flung open the French doors to greet Heather, squeezing her tightly. "I can't believe you're here. What do you think of the place? Have you had a look around?"

"Not yet. I was waiting for you to give me the grand tour," Heather said, following her sister inside.

"Good to see you again, Heather," Boyd said, embracing her. "Maybe Violet and I can take you out to dinner down by the river this evening."

"Sounds great. I just realized I forgot to eat the sandwich I brought for lunch," Heather answered with an embarrassed chuckle.

Violet shook her head. "Typical! Don't you ever take a break from work?" She linked her arm through Heather's and escorted her into the hallway. "Let's go on a walking tour right now. I'll show you everything we've done to the place."

After pointing out all the improvements on the ground floor, which included a new butler's pantry and fitness room, Violet led Heather upstairs to the expanded master suite replete with a private sitting room and walk-in closet half the size of Heather's condo.

"I just can't get over how big your closet is," she marveled. "It's bigger than most boutiques in LA."

Violet laughed. "Anything's big compared to LA quarters. Come on, I'll show you the guest room. And I don't want any discussion about where you're staying. You can bunk here with us for as long as you want." She ushered Heather into a bright, spacious room with a stunning view of the manicured back lawn and the river beyond.

"I love being this close to the water," Heather said in a wistful tone. "It reminds me of when we used to catch tadpoles together."

Violet joined her at the window. "You really should consider moving home. I know you miss this place, and I miss having you around." She took Heather's hand and sat down on the bed with her. "Most of all, I want my child to have a relationship with her aunt."

Heather's jaw dropped. "You're pregnant?"

Violet nodded coyly, her blue eyes glittering with joy. "It finally happened."

Heather hugged her, blinking back tears. Violet and Boyd had been trying for a baby for years. Recently, they'd been talking about adopting, and Heather had assumed they'd exhausted all avenues for a child of their own. "I'm so happy for you both," she said. "This is the best possible news."

"The icing on the cake would be to have you here," Violet responded. "You've always been there for me when I needed you in the past and—"

She broke off at a knock on the door. Boyd stepped inside, waving an envelope. "Sorry to interrupt," he said in a grim tone. "But I found this in the mail."

14

A chill ran up Heather's spine as Boyd walked toward her and Violet flapping an all-too-familiar-looking, pale blue envelope.

"What is it?" Violet asked, reaching out her hand for it.

Boyd frowned. "I don't want you getting upset over this, Violet. You know, with the ... " He caught himself midsentence and crinkled his forehead, his gaze flitting briefly to Heather. "Did you tell your sister our news?"

"If you mean about the baby, then yes, of course," Violet said impatiently. "Now stop fussing. Let me see what you've got there."

Boyd reluctantly handed her the envelope.

Violet slid the card out. "Pretty flowers!" she exclaimed.

Heather's stomach knotted. It was the exact same card she had received with a posy of forget-me-nots tied with burlap on the front.

A tiny furrow appeared on Violet's brow before she passed the card to Heather. "I'm not sure what to make of it."

Heather opened it and absorbed the words inside, her breath freezing in her throat.

You should be afraid.

She snapped the card shut, her brain whirring with new questions. Was Violet being targeted now too? Or did someone know she was staying here?

Violet tapped a finger on the picture. "Didn't you get a bouquet of forget-me-nots delivered to the reunion along with that prank message?"

Heather gave a vague nod. Violet thought she was here to help Marco investigate the arson. She hadn't told her yet that she'd received another threatening card back in LA. It was apparent by now that it was no prank, but she was reluctant to admit that to Violet. Especially now she knew she was pregnant.

"Do you think it's the same person?" Violet asked.

"It's possible," Heather replied, massaging her temples.

Boyd cleared his throat. "It can't be just a coincidence. I think we should take the card to the police."

Violet rolled her eyes. "Waste of time. They already know about the card at the reunion and they're not taking it seriously. They don't think it's connected to the arson."

"And they might be right," Heather said. "This could be someone harboring a petty grudge from high school. The arson, on the other hand, might have been a disgruntled employee, or teenagers messing around—who knows what." Heather pulled out her phone and took a photo of the card before handing it back to Violet. "Save this in case we need it down the line."

"We should probably take some steps to make this place more secure," Boyd said. "I don't like the idea of Violet being all alone in the house while I'm at work or off on a business trip with all this going on. She's not going to be able to travel with me as much now with the baby coming."

"I won't be alone," Violet said. "Heather's going to be staying here with us for the foreseeable future."

A flicker of unease crossed Boyd's face. "No offense, Heather, but that might only put Violet in more danger."

"Don't be ridiculous!" Violet protested, springing to her feet. "This is just some pathetic person whose life hasn't turned out the way they wanted it to, and they're jealous of Heather's success. Whatever it's about, she'll get to the bottom of it, and she's welcome to stay here until she does."

Boyd gave an unconvincing nod. "Let's hope you're right and we're only dealing with a harmless kook and not someone dangerous. I'm going to hit the shower before dinner."

"I need to run back to Marco's place and pick up the rest of my stuff," Heather said. "How about I meet you two at the restaurant?"

"Works for me. You girls decide where you want to go," Boyd said, exiting the room.

Violet reached for her phone. "I already know where I want to take you. I'm craving ribs tonight, and the Waterfront Bistro has the best smoked ribs you've ever tasted."

After securing a reservation for 7:00 p.m., Violet walked Heather out to her car. "You don't really think I have anything to be concerned about, do you?" She rubbed her belly affectionately. "It's not me I'm worried about—it's just with the baby coming and all."

"Of course not," Heather reassured her. "I'll figure this out and find the person who's behind it. Trust me, I'm an expert at tracking down lowlifes."

Violet's expression relaxed. "You've always been there for me, fighting my battles to the bitter end."

Heather forced a smile. Violet didn't know quite how

bitter the end had been to the battle that had changed their lives forever. And if Heather could help it, she never would.

As she drove back to Marco's place, she mulled over the latest message. She guessed it was intended for her—better that than someone was targeting Violet now too. Heather still couldn't rid herself of the suspicion that someone had found out what she'd done, but how? It was unthinkable that Lindsay could have betrayed her trust. The newspaper articles at the time hadn't mentioned anything about her car being spotted on the road that night. They had printed a picture of Damien Kinney— Tank as they had known him as—a few days after the accident, and then that was the end of it. Another foolhardy teenager lost to drunk driving.

When she pulled into the driveway, Anna was busy unloading groceries from the back of her SUV. Heather bit back her exasperation. She had hoped to grab her things and go, but it would be rude not to offer to help. She parked in front of the guest cottage and then walked back over to Anna's vehicle. "Here, let me take some of those for you," she offered.

Anna pulled a strand of hair out of her eyes and handed Heather a bag. "Thanks. My back's not what it used to be. I don't know how you keep so slim and trim. I keep piling on the pounds. To tell you the truth, I felt like a right hippo at the reunion."

"Nonsense!" Heather replied. "Marco couldn't keep his eyes off you."

Anna let out a snort as she reached into the trunk for another bag of groceries. "Couldn't keep his eyes *on* me, you mean."

Heather bit her lip, unsure of how to respond. Marco had made it sound as though he and Anna were getting on well now. Maybe there was some marital tiff going on behind the scenes.

"Oh, don't try and be so polite, Heather," Anna said, one hand on her hip. "I know all about his fling with Reagan. I'm sure you do too, so don't pretend otherwise. They think I don't know anything about it. I may not be college-educated like she is, but I'm not stupid either." She turned and huffed her way up the front steps, leaning her bag of groceries against the doorframe as she punched the entry code into the electronic keypad.

Heather followed her inside and down the hallway to the kitchen. Anna set the groceries on the kitchen table and turned to face her. "You did know about it, right?"

Heather inclined her head. "Reagan told me recently. I'm … sorry."

Anna waved a dismissive hand at her. "I knew they were carrying on behind my back. It wasn't just a fling, as they like to call it. It went on for the best part of a year. I thought about divorcing Marco when I first found out, but I couldn't put the kids through that—visitation, alternating holidays, not to mention a stepmother like Reagan. I shudder at the thought."

"Reagan thought her ex—Roy—might be behind the arson," Heather said. "Apparently, he knew about her and Marco too."

Anna glanced out the window, a faraway look in her eyes. "To be honest, I half-wondered if Reagan might have put Roy up to it."

Heather arched a surprised brow. "What makes you say that?"

Anna turned and held her gaze. "She wanted Marco to leave me—begged him to. I don't know if she was really in love with him, or if it was all about his money. She's got that jealous streak. You heard her snide comments at the reunion about my jewelry."

"How do you know she asked Marco to leave you?" Heather asked.

Anna shrugged. "I read their texts on his phone. Marco used our son's birthday as his passcode." She gave a rueful grin. "Maybe I should have been a PI."

"Good instincts are an asset," Heather acknowledged.

Anna's expression clouded over. "Sometimes I wish I didn't have such good instincts."

Heather gave her a sympathetic smile. "If it's any comfort, Reagan told me they both regretted it. It didn't mean anything to either one of them."

Anna threw her a funny look. "I'm not so sure about that. I've a hunch their connection went a whole lot deeper."

Before Heather could press her for more details, the back door opened and the kids burst into the kitchen, the clatter of soccer cleats echoing over the tile floor.

"Mom, I'm starving!"

"What's for dinner?"

"Can we have a snack, *please*?"

"I should go and let you guys eat," Heather said.

Marco followed the kids into the kitchen. "You're welcome to stay for dinner," he replied, tossing the soccer bags in the corner.

"Thanks, but I made plans with Violet and Boyd. They got back into town this afternoon, so I'm going to be staying with them now. I'm here to pick up my stuff."

Marco gave a distracted nod as he snatched a packet of cookies out of his youngest son's hands. "Not before dinner."

"Da-ad! I'm starving!" he whined.

"Have an apple," Marco said, before turning his attention back to Heather. "Did you make it out to Danny Baxter's place today?"

"I *hate* apples!" Marco's son growled, stomping his foot.

"Yeah, he's not your guy." Heather raised her voice to make herself heard above the ruckus. "I'll fill you in at dinner tomorrow night." She raised her hand in a parting wave to Anna and made a beeline for the front door.

On the drive to the Waterfront Bistro, Heather reflected on Anna's words. She hadn't got the impression from Reagan that she still had feelings for Marco. What kind of connection was Anna alluding to? Were Marco and Reagan business partners? Maybe Reagan had invested in the restaurants and wanted her money back out. That would explain why Anna suspected Reagan could be behind the arson. It seemed like a far-fetched theory, but Heather had seen it all over the years.

She pulled up at the Waterfront Bistro shortly before seven and made her way inside to where Violet and Boyd were seated at a table by the window.

"Wow! The view's amazing," Heather raved, peering out at the river, glittering orange under the restaurant's outdoor lights.

"Wait until you taste the ribs," Violet said, passing her a menu.

After making her selection, Heather spotted Sydney and Steve seated at the far end of the restaurant. "Order me the half rack of ribs," she said to Violet. "I'm just going to say hello to Sydney."

She ended up chatting for longer than she'd intended with Sydney and Steve, and by the time she returned to her table, her food had arrived. Smoky, charred to tender perfection, and coated in a hearty sweet and spicy sauce, the baby back ribs lived up to Violet's praise. When she was done, Heather licked her fingers and leaned back in her seat with a satisfied groan. "You can't find ribs like this in LA."

"Fall-off-the-bone deliciousness, and that sauce is to die for," Violet agreed. "Maybe now you'll consider moving back home."

Heather laughed. "You're not going to let up on that, are you?"

"Nope," Violet said. "My kid needs a hands-on aunt. Don't worry, I'll break you down eventually. You know how persistent I am."

"All right, let's get out of here," Boyd said, getting to his feet after signing the check. "I'm still on Boston time—about ready to hit the sack."

Fifteen minutes later, they slowed to a halt in the driveway. Spray-painted over the brick facade of Violet's and Boyd's gatepost was the word *KILLER*.

15

H eather jumped out of her car and joined Boyd and Violet to take a closer look at the freshly painted graffiti on the gatepost.

"It must be the same person who sent the card," Violet said, running her fingers over the red paint. "Whoever did this is more twisted than I thought."

"And more dangerous," Boyd added in a grim tone. "They must have been watching us leave. Pretty brazen of them to leave their signature on our property."

Heather shot him a startled look, but quickly masked her expression. It was better that Boyd believed that. The alternative—that someone was accusing Heather of being a killer—would be a whole lot harder to explain.

"I have no choice but to call the police now," Boyd said. "This is vandalism, plain and simple. It's gone way beyond hate mail from some ticked-off ex-classmate of yours, Heather."

Violet let out an exasperated sigh. "I still think you're wasting your time, honey. They won't do anything about it."

Heather held her tongue. Violet was right that it would accomplish nothing. It wasn't as if the police could do much more than file a report. But there was little she could do to talk Boyd out of it at this point. He wanted to protect Violet, and Heather understood where he was coming from only too well.

Fifteen minutes later, Heather found herself seated at the kitchen table with Violet, Boyd, and a baby-faced Detective Gates.

"You say you left the house at 6:45 p.m.?" the detective asked, wearing a somber expression more befitting a murder investigation. Heather felt sorry for him. He couldn't be more than twenty-two or twenty-three years old and he was doing his best to take a report of vandalism in an upscale neighborhood seriously. "What time did you return?"

"Oh, 9:30 p.m., or so," Violet replied. "I wanted to take a quick stroll along the river after dinner, but my husband wanted to get home."

Detective Gates rubbed his chin thoughtfully. "Um ... let's see ... that gives the perpetrator almost a three-hour window."

Heather caught Boyd's eye and raised her brows a fraction. He had the decency to look abashed. He knew as well as she did that this was a complete waste of time. They were simply going through the motions.

"Do you have any security cameras on the premises?" Detective Gates asked.

"Not down at the gate," Boyd answered. "We have them inside the house and along the eaves. I already checked, but no one came up the driveway while we were gone. All they really had to do was roll down a car window and spray the post in passing."

Detective Gates made a few notes. "Have you had any trouble like this before—kids messing around or anything of that nature?"

"No. This is a very safe neighborhood," Violet responded. "This wasn't the work of locals."

The detective gave a grave nod. "Could be a graffiti artist who goes by *Killer*. I'll ask around downtown."

"I wouldn't call the job artistic by any stretch of the imagination," Heather interjected, unable to curb her frustration any longer. "This is something more malevolent."

Detective Gates cleared his throat. "There's no accounting for taste when it comes to art these days," He directed a tiny frown in Heather's direction as if to remind her that he was interviewing the homeowners and didn't appreciate unsolicited input.

"There is one other thing," Violet said. She got up and rummaged through the mail she'd left lying on the kitchen counter. When she returned to the table, she handed Detective Gates the forget-me-not card. "I'm not sure if it's connected to the graffiti or not, but we just got this in the mail."

He flipped open the card and scanned the message inside. "Hmm. I'll make some inquiries and see if anyone else in the neighborhood has got any prank cards or graffitied messages on their gates or mailboxes. I suspect it's probably kids messing around. Halloween's only a few weeks away, after all." He snapped his notebook shut and got to his feet, throwing a lingering glance around the space. "Nice place you've got here."

"Thanks," Boyd replied, shaking the detective's hand before showing him to the front door.

"Halloween? Puh...lease!" Violet fumed, the minute

Boyd reappeared in the kitchen. "I warned you that would be a waste of time."

"At least it's on record now in case anything else happens." Boyd sat down heavily at the table and threw Heather a hopeful look. "Got any theories on who's behind the graffiti?"

Heather fought to keep her expression neutral. The theory that made the most sense was that this was about her. The card she'd received back in LA contained the word *killer*, too. But she was reluctant to divulge that to Boyd and Violet. It would lead to too many questions. She didn't want to lie to them, but she didn't want Violet to have to share the burden of her guilt over the terrible thing she'd done either. "I'm not sure, but I'm working my way through a list of suspects. We can rule out Marco's ex-employee, Danny Baxter, for starters. I visited him today and he's confined to a wheelchair. He had a work-related accident. I'm going to talk to the other people on the list and see what comes of it."

Violet yawned and stretched. "Time for me and little bean to turn in. We've had more than enough excitement for one night."

Boyd grunted his approval. "We could all do with a good night's sleep."

Heather retired to the guest room and pulled out her laptop. Between the card and the graffiti on the gatepost, she was worried that Boyd was right and her presence here was putting her sister in danger. She had to figure out what was going on and put an end to it. Marco and the rest of the group were expecting an update at dinner tomorrow night. She would begin by paring down the list of suspects they had given her. Resigned to the task at hand, she spent the next couple of hours researching the names on the list and tracking down their current contact details, and other pertinent information, before finally calling it a night.

After breakfast the following morning, she set out to pay a visit to Karen Hill, the ex-fiancée Sydney thought might still be pining after her husband, Steve. Karen was an unlikely suspect in Heather's estimation, but she was making a point of pursuing all the leads she'd been given.

It turned out Karen Hill ran a successful law practice and lived on a five-acre lot outside of Moline. Heather had considered texting or emailing her to alert her to her visit but decided against it. If Karen wasn't home, she would move on to the next person on the list and come back to her later. She pulled up outside the modern Colonial style house and grabbed her backpack off the seat. It never hurt to have a recording device on hand in case things took an unexpected turn. She rang the doorbell and listened to the Westminster chime resound throughout the house. A few minutes later, a petite woman with a sleek chestnut bob opened the door dressed in leggings and an over-sized sweatshirt. She looked Heather up and down and arched an amused brow. "I can't imagine what you're selling on a Sunday."

Heather smiled, warming to the woman's straightforward manner. "This isn't a sales call. My name's Heather Nelson. I'm a private investigator. I was friends with Sydney Duffy back in high school." After a heartbeat, she added. "She's Sydney McClintock now."

Karen's brows knitted together in a flicker of a frown before she gestured for Heather to come inside. "I just brewed a pot of coffee. My husband took the kids on a bike ride. He didn't want to let them go on their own after what happened to that poor girl Lindsay ... whatshername."

"Robinson," Heather offered, sitting down on a leather stool at the kitchen counter while Karen poured the coffee.

"You saw the article then. Very sad story," Karen said, filling a small jug with creamer.

"I knew her well. She was a good friend of mine. She was on the student council with me back in high school—and Sydney too, of course," Heather said, trying to steer the conversation back around to the purpose of her visit.

"Cream and sugar?" Karen asked.

"Just black for me, thanks."

Karen joined her at the counter and handed her a steaming mug of coffee. "I'm sorry about your friend. Is that why you're here? You mentioned you're a private investigator."

Heather took a sip of coffee before responding. "Not exactly. This has more to do with Sydney. You seem like a straight shooter, so I'll get to the point. Something rather unsettling happened at our twentieth high school reunion last month. Our student council table got a delivery of flowers with a disturbing message on the accompanying card: *you deserve to die.*"

Karen's discriminating eyes narrowed. "That's a nasty thing to happen."

"It definitely put a damper on things," Heather agreed. "Anyway, as I do this kind of thing for a living, the others asked me to dig around a little and find out if anyone from our high school days still had a beef with us about something. We're not sure if the message was aimed at one of us, or all of us."

Karen raised her brows, an amused grin dancing on her lips. "Let me guess, Sydney suggested I might be behind it?"

Heather gave an apologetic shrug. "As you can imagine, I'm in a difficult position. I promised my friends I would follow up with anyone they thought might be holding a grudge."

Karen threw back her head and laughed. "Not me! To tell you the truth, I have to thank Sydney for taking Steve off my hands. If she hadn't, I might never have met my husband, Brian. He's a corporate lawyer too. We make a good team." She gestured to a frame on the wall. "That's the most recent family photo of us. Those are our kids, Sasha and Henry."

"You have a beautiful family," Heather said, with a tight-lipped smile—quashing an unexpected pang of jealousy.

"Thank you. I'm very blessed."

"I should get going. I've taken up enough of your time," Heather said. "I'm sorry to interrupt your Sunday morning with something this banal."

"Don't worry about it," Karen said, setting down her mug. "I get that you're trying to help your friends. Sydney's a nice girl, and I don't bear her any ill-will. Between you and me, I doubt the message is targeted at her."

Heather got to her feet and carried her mug over to the sink. "I'm sure you're right. I'll let her know you're not harboring any unresolved grudges."

Karen accompanied Heather to the door. "You might want to leave out the part about me thanking her for marrying Steve," she said with a wry grin. "She might think I'm insulting her."

Heather laughed. "You can count on it." She waved goodbye and strode down the path. She had a feeling she would enjoy working with Karen Hill if circumstances were different and she had never left Iowa.

Back in her car, she dialed Sydney's number, eager to put her mind at rest. The phone rang several times before a harried voice answered, "This is Steve."

"Hey, Steve. It's Heather. I'm just leaving Karen Hill's house and I wanted to fill Sydney in on our conversation. Is she available?"

"She can't come to the phone right now. She's really sick. I think it's food poisoning."

16

Alarm bells went off immediately in Heather's head. In light of everything else going on, it seemed like a strange coincidence that Sydney had suddenly come down with a case of food poisoning. On the other hand, she didn't want to cause Steve any undue concern by voicing her suspicions prematurely. "I'm sorry to hear that. When did she come down with it?"

"Just a few minutes ago," Steve said, sounding frazzled. "She went out to pick us up some lattes and she complained about feeling nauseous and dizzy on the way home. She's blaming the oysters we had last night. I was just about to call the Waterfront Bistro and ask if anyone else was affected, although I'm pretty sure she would have felt sick before now." He hesitated before continuing, "You don't think this could have anything to do with the messages, do you? It's just with the arson, and Reagan getting cut off on the freeway, and now this—I'm really worried. I want her to go to the ER and get checked out, but she thinks I'm overreacting. I probably am, it's just disconcerting. Sorry, I know I'm rambling."

"I doubt it's related," Heather said. "Whoever sent the messages would have no way of knowing when or where you were going out to eat, and no way of tampering with your food."

"No, you're right, of course." He gave a nervous laugh. "We've been a bit on edge ever since the arson."

Heather drummed her fingers lightly on the steering wheel. She hadn't decided yet if she was going to tell the others at dinner about the graffiti and the card that had been sent to Violet's address. It would almost certainly heighten their fears, and—what was worse—it would turn the spotlight on her.

"Maybe you can let Sydney know I called and that everything's good with Karen," Heather said. "I hope she feels better soon. If she can't make dinner tonight, I'll be sure to email her with an update on everything we discuss."

Heather hung up, her thoughts racing in several different directions at once. Even though she'd assured Steve that the food poisoning would be unrelated to what was going on, she couldn't help wondering if that was actually the case. She kept circling back to Lindsay's bizarre death. It had all begun there. She couldn't shake the feeling that there was some underlying connection she was missing. The strange hook she'd found in the brush still bothered her too. But was she reading too much into it? It could have been lying there from before the accident, for all she knew.

Pushing the conundrum to the back of her mind for now, she opened up Google Maps on her phone. There was one more name on the list she wanted to visit before meeting up with the others at dinner. Dan Wilcox was the bereaved husband of Josh's patient—the ex-model he had more or less admitted to being attracted to. Heather didn't particularly relish the prospect of interviewing the grieving husband. Words were wholly inadequate in these kinds of situations. But he had threatened Josh, so she had to make sure he could be eliminated as a suspect.

Thirty minutes later, she pulled up outside a picturesque farmhouse set against a backdrop of fields mantled with corn swaying gently in a light breeze. She had emailed Dan Wilcox earlier and explained she was writing a book on the god-complex among psychiatrists, and that she had heard about his wife's suicide and wanted to know more about her story. Dan had readily agreed to an interview. Whether or not he was behind the messages, it was clear from his response that he harbored considerable anger and resentment toward Josh.

He opened the front door as Heather was walking up the stamped concrete pathway. She could tell by the listless, glassy look in his eyes that he'd been drinking, even though it was early in the afternoon. Evidently, he wasn't coping well with his wife's untimely death. "You must be Dan," she said, extending a hand in greeting.

He shook it limply and ushered her inside to a tasteful kitchen with cherry wood cabinetry and oil-rubbed bronze fixtures. The granite counters were littered with miscellaneous items and the sink was full of dirty dishes. A small stack of used paper plates sat atop the table and the trash can was overflowing. Dan Wilcox appeared to have lost the plot since his wife's demise in more ways than one.

"Thanks for agreeing to see me on such short notice," Heather began. "As I explained in my email, my deadline's looming, and I only need two more stories to supplement the research I've done on this important topic."

Dan ran a hand through his tousled hair. "I should have filed a malpractice suit. I wanted to, believe me, but Ruby's family talked me out of it. They didn't want the whole world knowing the sordid story. I think they were afraid the media would turn her into a sideshow—her being a model and all."

"What type of modeling did she do—catwalk, magazines?"

He sniffed, pinching his brows together. "A bit of both, back in the day. Ruby had gone as far as she could in her modeling career. She was never going to make it to the big time. I think she'd finally realized that, but she took it hard. That's when the depression set in. Modeling was really the only dream she ever had."

"How did you two meet?" Heather asked.

"We were high school sweethearts. I was captain of the football team and she was a cheerleader." He twisted his lips into a regretful smile. "Same old cliché."

Heather made a show of writing something down in the notebook she'd brought with her. "How long had she been going to counseling for her depression?"

"About six months or so." Dan's face darkened. "If I'd had any idea what was going on in that office behind closed doors between her and Josh Halverson, I'd have pulled the plug on it a long time ago."

"So do you think Ruby began to latch onto her doctor—transference, I believe they call it?" Heather asked, scribbling it down and underlining it. "It's a common thread in all the stories I'm documenting."

Dan's eyes glittered with hate as he leaned forward in his chair. "I blame him for what happened. He had her completely under his control. Ruby was sick—she wasn't thinking straight. She came home one day and told me she was in love with him and wanted a divorce. Who do you think planted that idea in her head?"

Heather painted on a perturbed frown. "That must have made you feel so helpless."

"That's the problem with these doctors," Dan fumed. "They have too much power over vulnerable people like Ruby. He had access to all her mental health records. I was out of the loop. I only knew what she told me. Somebody needs to hold these doctors accountable. I bet she wasn't the only one he took advantage of. There's usually a pattern with these kinds of people." He waved his hand angrily through the air, getting visibly more worked up by the minute. "Just like that doctor who abused all those Olympic gymnasts. It went on for years and no one blew the whistle on that lowlife."

Heather nodded along in agreement. "So, in your opinion, Dan, what's the public supposed to do?"

"That's the real question, isn't it? What do you do when you can't get justice?" He scowled and rubbed a hand over his knuckles, his gaze drilling into her.

Heather swallowed, trying to hide the fact that her hand was shaking. If only he knew how well she could relate to the emotions roiling around inside him.

"I'll tell you what happens," Dan growled. "When people get sick and tired of being sick and tired, they take matters into their own hands."

Heather arched a questioning brow. "And how do you feel about that?"

Dan folded his arms over his chest. "I say good on them. Somebody needs to do what needs to be done."

Heather gave an enthusiastic nod. "That's a great quote, *somebody needs to do what needs to be done.* Do you mind if I use that in the book?"

Dan pulled his brows together in momentary confusion as if he'd suddenly remembered the purpose of her visit. "Don't put my name after it. Next thing you know, he'll be suing me for threatening him or something. I want to remain an anonymous source, you understand."

Heather bent over her notebook and jotted a few things down. For all his bluster and bravado, Dan was a coward—which cast considerable doubt on the idea that he was behind the threatening messages, let alone the arson. "I think that's enough for me to go on for now," Heather said, closing her notebook. "If I think of anything else, I'll email you. I appreciate your time, Dan."

"You're lucky you caught me," he said, getting to his feet. "I've been fishing in Montana for the past week. We slayed them."

Heather raised her brows. "Lucky indeed," she said, hurrying to the door before he could launch into a prolonged fishing story.

Back in her car, she crossed Dan Wilcox off her shrinking list. She would verify the fishing trip, of course—she was a professional, after all—but he had no reason to lie to her. She checked the clock in the car and made a quick calculation. There was still time before dinner to make one more stop. It might be worth driving by Roy's place again to see if he was home. She made a U-turn on the road and drove back out to the subdivision where he lived, slowing down as she approached the house. A woman in skinny, ripped jeans and a baggy V-necked sweater was standing at the bottom of the driveway, one hand on her hip as she watched a toddler pushing a plastic tricycle around. Was this Roy's wife and child? Reagan hadn't mentioned anything about a family, but maybe she didn't know about them. Heather pulled over and switched off the engine. She observed the woman from a distance for a few minutes before climbing out of her car and approaching her. "Hi," she called out with a friendly wave. "I'm looking for Roy Krueger. Does he live here?"

The woman's heavily lined eyes narrowed as she sized up Heather. "Who's asking?"

"My name's Janis Wells. I'm a clerk at the law offices of Bodensteiner and Kern," she said, pulling a file out of her backpack and holding it up. "We're trying to track down any living relatives of Roy Krueger."

A flicker of interest crossed the woman's face. She cast a quick glance at her son who was still peddling around in circles singing to himself, oblivious to the adult conversation. "You're out of luck," the woman said. "Roy's at work. Or so he says."

"Are you his wife?"

The woman made a disgruntled sound. "He has yet to put a ring on my finger. I'm Aidy."

Heather gestured to the little boy. "Cute kid. What's his name?"

"This is Trevor." Aidy pulled a face. "Everyone says he takes after Roy's side of the family." She threw a curious look at the file folder in Heather's hand. "Does Roy have some money coming to him or something?"

Heather cocked her head to one side. "That's what we're trying to determine. We need to gather some more information. Roy didn't respond to our email so I'm pursuing it in person."

"Let's hope it's a big fat inheritance." Aidy patted her stomach. "It couldn't come at a better time. Our second child's due in April."

Heather assumed a puzzled expression and flipped open the file folder, making a show of checking her information.

"I may be mistaken, but it was my understanding that Roy had an older daughter also."

The woman folded her arms across her chest and smirked. "He thought he did for the longest time. But she's not his, is she?"

17

H eather got back in her car and pulled out of the cul-de-sac where Roy lived, headed for Marco's restaurant. Aidy's words tumbled around inside her head like lottery balls in a raffle drum, each new combination offering a less satisfactory explanation than the one before. Heather had tried to press her for more details about Lucy, but Aidy had clammed up and told her to talk to Roy about it. Heather left her number with her and asked her to call when Roy returned. After that, Aidy steered Trevor's tricycle back up the driveway and disappeared around the side of the house—the little boy wailing in protest.

Heather mulled over the ambiguous comment as she drove. If Lucy wasn't Roy's child, then whose child was she? Was Reagan hiding even more of a checkered past than she had divulged? Heather chewed on her lip, considering another possibility that took her breath away. What if Lucy was Marco's daughter? As earth-shattering a thought as it was, it would explain Anna's cryptic comment the day before: *I've a hunch their connection went a whole lot deeper.*

From Heather's perspective, it changed the dynamics of

the investigation. If Anna had put two and two together, she might be behind the arson herself. She could be trying to pin it on Reagan to get back at Marco, covering her tracks by threatening the other members of the student council too. It was a clever strategy—timing it to coincide with the class reunion and casting suspicion on Marco's former classmates. But Heather would have to tread carefully pursuing that theory. She would need to be very sure of her facts before she accused Marco's own wife of setting his restaurant ablaze.

She pulled into The Sardinian parking lot and sat in her car for several minutes, not wanting to be the first one seated alone at the table with Marco. She wasn't sure she could look him in the eye knowing she was keeping something this substantial from him. Then again, maybe Marco knew the truth about Lucy. He might even be giving Reagan money to support her. As fast as the plot was thickening, Heather's trust in her former classmates was eroding.

Out of the corner of her eye, she spotted Josh pulling into the parking lot, Reagan right behind him. She waited for a few minutes and then followed them inside. The hostess escorted her to the private room at the back of the restaurant where they'd met for dinner the first night.

"Hey guys!" Heather said, nodding to the others. Josh mumbled something in response and exchanged an uneasy glance with Marco. Reagan raised a water glass to her lips, averting her gaze. Heather frowned, picking up on the strained atmosphere. Her thoughts gravitated at once to Sydney.

"What's wrong?" She pulled out a chair and joined them at the table. "Has Sydney taken a turn for the worse?"

Marco fixed a steely gaze on her, his jaw moving side-to-side, as if contemplating whether to break some unwelcome news to her.

Heather looked from Josh to Reagan, the skin on the back of her neck prickling. "Will someone please tell me what's going on?"

"Fine!" Reagan blurted out. "*I'll* tell her." She dug around in her purse and pulled out a forget-me-not card, slapping it down on the table in front of Heather. "Another message came in the mail today."

"We all got it," Josh added quietly.

Heather reached for the card and opened it, her stomach twisting as she read the words.

Heather has killed before. She'll do it again. You don't know her.

"Any idea what this means?" Reagan asked curtly.

Josh glared across the table at her. "What kind of a question is that?"

"It's a pretty straightforward one," Reagan snapped. "Let her answer it."

Heather handed the card back to her, making a concerted effort to exude a calmness she didn't feel inside. "It doesn't mean anything. It's a tactic to turn us against one another. Evidently, it's working." She threw an accusatory gaze at Reagan.

"Well you have to admit, this changes things," Reagan huffed. "I mean, it's your name on the card, Heather. This makes it about you."

Josh let out an exasperated sigh. "Cut it out, Reagan! It's just like Heather said. Whoever's doing this is trying to rile us up and divide us."

Marco scrunched his dark, bushy brows together. "The card's hogwash, just like the other ones. We all know

Heather's not a killer. We can't take the ramblings of a nutcase seriously."

Reagan pursed her lips, her pinched expression suggesting she wasn't convinced.

Josh turned to Heather. "Did you find out anything useful today?"

Heather pulled out the list of suspects and glanced at it. "We can eliminate Marco's ex-employee for starters. Danny Baxter is wheelchair-bound—has been ever since a work-related accident in a warehouse a few months back."

Marco scratched his stubble. "That's rough. I never liked the guy, but I wouldn't have wished that on him."

"Could he have hired someone to set the fire?" Josh asked.

Heather twisted her lips. "I'd say it's unlikely. He couldn't even remember the name of the restaurant. He didn't strike me as someone fixated on revenge—he didn't mention Marco the whole time."

"Strike him off the list," Marco said. "Who's next?"

"Karen Hill. She was engaged to Sydney's husband, Steve. We can rule her out too. She and her husband are successful lawyers. I took the direct approach with her—told her about the flower delivery at the reunion and explained that we were trying to figure out who had sent it. She actually laughed when I told her Sydney had given me her name as a possible suspect. She was thankful Sydney had taken Steve off her hands." Heather gave a wry grin. "Although she did ask me not to tell Sydney that. She didn't want to offend her."

Marco reached for the open bottle of wine on the table and refilled his glass. "Okay, so Karen Hill's not our psycho stalker. Next?"

Heather met his eyes briefly before glancing away.

Anna was the next person she'd spoken to, and she'd raised a few red flags, but she wasn't an official suspect. For now, Heather would have to keep her thoughts on that topic to herself. "Next is Roy Krueger. I've gone by his house a couple of times, but I haven't managed to connect with him, yet." She hesitated before pinning her gaze on Reagan. "I did manage to talk to Aidy, the mother of his child."

Reagan blinked in apparent confusion. "News to me that he has another child." She gave an offhand shrug. "I haven't been keeping tabs on him."

Heather arched a brow but said nothing. Reagan's body language told her she was lying through her teeth. Was it possible she still had feelings for Roy?

"Did you learn anything from Aidy?" Josh asked.

Heather allowed a long pause to unfold while she observed Reagan's demeanor. She was agitated but working hard to appear nonchalant. "Not really," Heather replied. "But it seems unlikely that Roy's involved—he has a whole new life. No offense, Reagan, but he doesn't appear to be pining for you."

Reagan tossed her head. "Doesn't mean to say he's not fueled up on enough hatred to try and run me off the freeway."

Marco shot her a dark look as he reached for a piece of bread and dipped it in oil. "Who else is on the list?"

"Dan Wilcox," Heather answered.

Marco frowned. "And he is?"

"His wife was my patient," Josh explained. "She's the one who committed suicide."

"Did you talk to him?" Reagan asked.

Heather gave a circumspect nod. "He's struggling to cope with his wife's death. He's still very angry about it, but, honestly, I can't see him being behind what's going on. He's turned to alcohol to drown his sorrows."

"So who does that leave us with?" Marco asked.

"We're basically back to Roy," Heather replied. "Unless you've come up with anyone else?"

Marco pinched the bridge of his nose. "Reagan, did you get Heather that list of everyone who worked on the reunion committee with us?"

"I have it right here," Reagan said, pulling out her phone. She frowned at the screen and let out a gasp. "Oh no! Sydney's at the hospital."

Heather's stomach lurched. Her fears that Sydney had something more than a straightforward case of food poisoning came rushing back with a vengeance.

"Steve says he took her to ER this morning," Reagan went on, reading snippets from the text. "She was throwing up and dizzy ... slurring her words ... having difficulty breathing ... stable now but they're running some tests."

"Tests?" Marco echoed. "What kind of tests? I thought she had food poisoning."

"I don't know," Reagan said.

"We should go to the hospital and check up on her," Josh suggested. "This might have something to do with what's going on."

Reagan let out a horrified bleat as she scrambled to her feet. "Are you saying she was poisoned?"

"We don't know that," Heather cut in. "There's no sense in speculating until the test results come back."

"I'll drive," Marco said, pulling out his car keys. "You can leave your vehicles here."

Heather gestured for the keys. "How about the teetotaler among us takes the wheel?"

· · ·

Steve was hunched over in a chair next to Sydney's bed when they got to her room on the fourth floor of the hospital.

"How's she doing?" Reagan asked, squeezing him lightly on the shoulder.

He gave a weak smile. "They pumped her stomach, and they had to put her on oxygen. She was having difficulty breathing." He rubbed a hand over his jaw, a haggard expression on his face. "To be honest, it was touch and go for a while. She had a seizure. Her parents got here a couple of hours ago. They're down in the cafeteria."

"It doesn't sound like food poisoning," Heather said. "What do the doctors think is wrong with her?"

Steve flapped a hand helplessly. "They contacted the restaurant, but they haven't given me an update. Supposedly, they're still waiting on the test results."

Heather glanced up as a young olive-skinned doctor strode into the room. He pushed his glasses up his nose and nodded around at everyone before addressing Steve. "Mr. McClintock, we have your wife's test results." He hesitated before adding, "We'd like to discuss them with you in private."

Steve blinked, a look of confusion clouding his face as two detectives entered the room.

18

Reagan cast a wary glance over her shoulder before hurrying into The Sardinian. After they'd arrived back from the hospital, Heather had taken off to drive by Roy's house again. Reagan immediately texted Josh and Marco and asked them to meet her back inside. All thoughts of finishing dinner had vanished after learning that Sydney had been poisoned with ethylene glycol—a chemical found in antifreeze. The detectives had questioned Steve at length about Sydney's movements that morning and wanted to know everything she'd consumed since dinner the previous evening. It was apparent they considered Steve a suspect, but Reagan had another theory to run by Marco and Josh.

"So, what's this about?" Josh asked, pulling out a chair and joining her and Marco at the table. "It's late. Was it really so important it couldn't wait?"

Reagan flashed him a steely look. "*Obviously*. Otherwise I wouldn't have asked you to meet me back here. We need to have a conversation without Heather around so we can speak freely."

Marco frowned. "Doesn't she need to be here too? She's the one investigating this."

"That's what's freaking me out," Reagan said. "That card we got about her *killing before* and *she'll do it again. You don't know who she really is.* What if it's all true? After all, we haven't seen her in years. What do we actually know about her? Think about it for a minute. What if Heather's behind everything that's going on?"

Josh shook his head in disgust. "How can you insinuate something like that? That's messed up, Reagan. What reason would Heather have for wanting to kill us?"

"I don't know, but that's my point," Reagan said, jabbing a finger in his direction. "We don't know anything about her. She's been gone out of our lives for years. She could have been in prison all this time for all we know."

"Give me a break! She wouldn't be able to work as a PI with a prison record," Marco growled.

"And that's another thing," Reagan went on. "We don't know if her grandiose PI career in LA is real. She could have made the whole thing up. Did she even go back to LA after the reunion? Maybe we should hire a PI to follow *her* around."

"You're being ridiculous," Josh said. "You got her contact info off her website for crying out loud."

Reagan pursed her lips. "Okay, so maybe it is a legitimate career. It still doesn't mean to say she isn't behind everything that's happening. She has experience with the criminal world, she knows better than any of us how to get away with this kind of thing. I think we should confront her."

"Confront her about what exactly? She hasn't done anything. Where's this coming from all of a sudden?" Josh demanded, his voice rising.

Reagan reached for her wine glass with shaking fingers

and took a hasty sip. "I'm just trying to figure out why she agreed to come to the reunion when she hasn't been back to Iowa in twelve years."

"She came for Lindsay, not us," Josh pointed out.

"He's right," Marco added. "What motive does Heather have for threatening us anonymously?"

Reagan gave a defensive shrug. "Maybe she still resents the fact that she didn't become class president. Remember how mad she was at you guys for voting for me instead of her? She even accused me of bribing students to get her vote and spreading rumors about her."

"Come on, Reagan. We're all adults now," Josh said. "Heather's got better things to do than pine over some silly high school position."

Reagan arched a brow at him. "There's nothing silly about being elected president of the student council. And you can't deny she got all weird after I won."

Josh turned to Marco. "I think it's about time we shut this down. It's late and we're all tired and on edge."

"Verging on hysterical," Marco muttered.

"Look, I'm not saying Heather's behind this," Reagan snapped. "I just think it's worth considering the possibility. She's made a career out of hunting people down and—"

"Not just any people. Bad guys, Reagan," Marco cut in, shaking his head at her. "She hunts bad guys for a living. Not her former classmates who ticked her off when she was seventeen."

"She could be unstable," Reagan countered. "Let's face it, her life isn't exactly normal. She's never been married, or engaged, never even been in a serious relationship. She's a loner, works nights. All red flags if you ask me. I think we should hire someone to trail her and see what she's really up to."

"Just because she doesn't lead your tidy little suburban life doesn't mean she's a killer," Josh said. "She's always been upfront about the fact that she's married to her work. So are lots of other people who aren't killers. It's not like she's hiding anything from us." He glanced from Reagan to Marco. "Maybe we should take a long hard look at each other. You both act like you've got something to hide at times. You bicker like an old married couple. If you have anything to say, now's the time to come clean."

Marco's eyes glinted. "What's that supposed to mean?"

"Exactly what I said," Josh barked back.

Marco shot Reagan a guarded look. "I haven't got anything to hide, do you?"

Reagan wet her lips, her heart pounding in her chest. "Don't be stupid. Let's circle back to Heather. Don't you think it's a bit too much of a coincidence that she ate at the same restaurant as Sydney and Steve last night, and even sat at their table for a while?"

"You're not suggesting Heather poisoned Sydney, are you?" Josh scoffed.

Marco scratched his jaw. "Reagan does have a point. This wasn't an accidental ethylene glycol poisoning on the restaurant's part. No one else got sick, which means someone got close enough to Sydney to doctor her drink or food."

"How about we call Violet, and see what she has to say?" Reagan suggested. "She was at the restaurant last night too. Heather gave me her number in case I needed to get a hold of her."

"How's that supposed to work?" Josh asked, rubbing his brow. "Hey Violet, we're worried your sister might be trying to kill us."

Reagan flashed him an icy glare. "It's about time you

started taking this seriously. Sydney could have died today. Violet might know something—after all, Heather's staying with her. We just need a legitimate reason to call. We can say we're worried about Heather, that the latest card really upset her, and we want to make sure she's all right."

Marco shrugged. "Fire away."

Josh grimaced. "I'm not in favor of it, but I can't stop you if you insist."

Reagan wasted no time pulling out her phone and dialing. When Violet picked up, she hit the speaker button. "Hey Violet, it's Reagan here."

"Oh, hi, Reagan. Are you trying to reach Heather?"

"Actually, it's you I wanted to talk to. We just got back from the hospital. Turns out Sydney was poisoned."

There was an audible gasp on the other end of the line. "Is Heather with her right now?"

"No. She went by my ex's house again. She wanted to try and catch him before she headed back to your place." Reagan cleared her throat. "The thing is, Violet, between you and me, I'm worried about Heather. Those cards we got in the mail today really unsettled her."

"The *you should be afraid* one? I got it too," Violet said.

Reagan frowned. "Ours had a different message. It mentioned Heather specifically. Didn't she tell you?"

"No, she never said anything about it. I think she's trying not to scare me. Did someone threaten her again?"

"Quite the opposite. Someone was warning us about her," Reagan replied.

There was a loaded pause before Violet asked, "What was the message?"

"*Heather has killed before. She'll do it again. You don't know her.*"

"That's sick!" Violet raged. "Whoever's behind this must

know that Heather's investigating them. They're trying to throw you off the trail."

Reagan let out an exaggerated sigh. "I'm sure you're right. But I think it's starting to get to Heather. That's why I wanted to ask you how she's doing with all of this. You know her best."

"I'm not sure how to answer that, to be honest," Violet said. "We used to be really close—we talked about everything—but I've only seen Heather a handful of times since she left Iowa, and only when I went out to visit her in LA."

"She told me she doesn't have any friends out there she can confide in," Reagan said. "That seems strange after living in LA for the best part of two decades."

"I know, right?" Violet sighed. "She kind of retreated into herself after high school and became laser focused on her work. I can't deny she excels at it, but she's a bit of a loner. Her dog, Phoebe, is about the only company she has. I think she regrets letting her friendship with Lindsay slide over the years. Granted, Lindsay was busy competing all over the country, but Heather could have made more of an effort to go to some of her races. I told her so a bunch of times. It's good she's been able to reconnect with you, even though it came about through unfortunate circumstances."

"We're all grateful she agreed to come back and investigate what's happening," Reagan said. "We kind of drifted apart in our last year in high school. We both ran for class president, as you know—I think she resented me for winning. Hopefully, that's all water under the bridge now."

"I'm sure she doesn't hold it against you," Violet said. "She certainly hasn't said anything to that effect."

"That's reassuring to hear. I'd hate to think—" Reagan broke off when Marco let out a raucous sneeze.

"What was that?" Violet asked, an edge to her voice. "Is someone there with you?"

"No, not really. I'm at The Sardinian."

"Is Marco there?" Violet demanded.

"Well, yes. But—"

Violet cut her off. "Let me guess, Josh is listening in too. Is that what this is really about? Are you guys ganging up on Heather behind her back? Do you honestly think she's some kind of sick killer, or what?"

"Calm down, Violet!" Reagan soothed, grimacing across the table at Josh and Marco.

"And to think I actually thought you were being sympathetic for once," Violet sputtered. "All the while you're pumping me for information. Well let me tell you something, you've got all the information you're going to get out of me. And you better believe I'm going to be telling Heather about this call and how you're scheming behind her back— just like you did in high school, bribing everyone to vote for you and spreading your poisonous rumors. I know what you're up to, but this time, you won't get away with sabotaging my sister!"

19

Heather pulled onto the street where Roy lived and switched off the engine. The house was in darkness and there were no vehicles parked in the driveway or along the curb. It was only 8:30 p.m.—too early for Roy and Aidy to have turned in for the night. Heather drummed her fingers on the steering wheel. She could afford to hang around for an hour or two before heading back to Violet's place. She reclined her seat a few inches and fished a water bottle out of her backpack.

Her thoughts gravitated to Sydney. Test results had confirmed ethylene glycol poisoning—a sobering diagnosis. There was little doubt in Heather's mind now that this was connected to the threatening messages. The police had grilled Steve for a good half hour, wanting to know if Sydney had had any suicidal thoughts, how stable their relationship was, whether they had got into an argument that morning, if they kept antifreeze in their garage—on and on until an already emotional Steve had been on the verge of tears. Heather couldn't help wondering what the police would think if they knew about the cards accusing her of being a killer. Would Steve suspect her of poisoning Sydney once he opened his mail? After all, she had sat at their table chatting with them for a good ten minutes last night at the restaurant —more than enough time to slip something into her drink.

After casting another glance up and down the street, Heather retrieved her phone from her purse and pulled up a website detailing the various signs and stages of ethylene glycol poisoning. Odorless, and colorless, it was a not uncommon method of poisoning in domestic murder cases. It came as no surprise to read that alcoholics sometimes killed themselves by ingesting it with anti-freeze. Disturbingly, children had even been known to drink it due to its sweet taste. Heather furrowed her brow as she scanned the rest of the article. Sydney had exhibited many of the classic symptoms of ethylene glycol poisoning: slurred speech, dizziness, headache, nausea, vomiting, difficulty in breathing. Thankfully, Steve had overruled her reluctance to seek medical help and insisted on taking her to the ER. If she had stayed home, kidney failure would have been a real danger, and by then it would have been too late.

The real question in Heather's mind, and no doubt in the minds of the detectives, was how Sydney had ingested the poison. She felt fairly confident that she could rule out the Waterfront Bistro. According to the website, Sydney would have been experiencing symptoms almost right away. That only left two possibilities in Heather's mind. Either Steve had slipped the poison to her, or someone had added it to the latte she had picked up at the coffee shop. But how could anyone have tampered with her drink in a public space? It seemed the more unlikely option, which left the chilling possibility that Steve was the culprit.

Heather leaned her head against the car window and stared across at Roy's house, still shrouded in darkness. She would give it another fifteen minutes and then call it a night and try again tomorrow. Something told her Roy wasn't the key to everything that was happening, beginning with Lindsay's bizarre death. This was bigger than the bad blood between Roy and Reagan.

Turning her attention back to her phone, she opened her browser and typed in: *what does it feel like to die from a rattlesnake bite?* For several minutes, she stared at the page of results that came up, loathe to click on an article and read the morbid details. But another part of her needed to know what Lindsay's last moments on earth had been like. Gritting her teeth, Heather clicked on the first article and began reading.

Typically, you will experience pain, tingling, or burning in the area where you've been bitten. Swelling, bruising, or discoloration at the site is common.

Heather squirmed in her seat. In Lindsay's case, the swelling and discoloration had been severe—so severe that her mother had chosen to have her cremated. Heather blew out a shaky breath. It must have been traumatic for Pam to have to identify her daughter. It was still hard for Heather to fathom that Lindsay had been bitten twice—it was extremely unusual. The coroner had speculated that Lindsay had landed on, or close to, a nest of rattlesnakes or possibly a breeding pair.

Heather glanced back down at her phone screen and scrolled through the progression of symptoms: *numbness in the face or limbs, lightheadedness, weakness, nausea or vomiting, sweating, blurred vision, difficulty breathing.* Not unlike Sydney's symptoms. She exited out of her browser and tossed her phone into the console, her stomach lurching. It was horrific to picture Lindsay slowly dying at the side of the trail as night fell, suffering, and all alone. None of it made sense. Lindsay had been an elite athlete and a professional cyclist. What could have caused her to crash on what for her was a basic trail?

Heather glanced across the street one last time, and then started up the car. It was getting late and she was cold and tired—time to head back to Violet's. She had stuck around long enough for the elusive Roy to make an appearance. Her meeting with Reagan's ex would have to wait for another day.

As soon as she walked into Violet's kitchen, she could tell by the expression on her sister's face that she was upset about something.

"Where have you been?" Violet asked.

Heather flopped down on the chair next to her. "I drove by Roy's place and hung out for a while. You weren't worried about me, were you?"

Violet pressed her lips into a tight line. "I'm more worried about you now than ever."

Heather raised her brows a fraction. "Has something happened?"

"You could say that," Violet retorted, folding her arms on the table in front of her.

"Are you going to make me pull it out of you, or can you just spare me the agony and tell me what's bothering you?"

"Your so-called *friends* are what's bothering me."

Heather spread her hands in a gesture of helplessness. "You've lost me."

"Reagan called me a little while ago. She said she wanted to talk to me about you. All very hush hush. She tried to make out she was concerned about your mental health and the strain you were under investigating what was going on."

Heather gave a small shrug. "That's typical Reagan. Always trying to take control and manage the situation."

"That wasn't it at all. She was on a fishing expedition."

"What do you mean?"

Violet narrowed her eyes. "She wanted to know how you reacted to the card: *Heather has killed before. She'll do it again. You don't know her*—the card you neglected to tell me about."

Heather sighed and smoothed her hair back from her face. "I didn't want you worrying about me any more than you already are."

"Bit late for that," Violet huffed.

"What else did Reagan ask you?"

"She wanted to know if you still resented the fact that she was elected class president. She thinks you're harboring a grudge against the rest of the student council for voting for her—that you're behind everything that's going on. Doesn't that bother you? That your *friends* think you're some kind of psycho loner who has come back twelve years later to bump them off."

Heather stared at her aghast. "It's just Reagan over-reacting—"

"It's not just Reagan," Violet interrupted. "Josh and Marco were sitting right there with her listening in on every word while she was pretending to have a private conversation with me. All the while, she was milking me for information about you—asking about your life in LA."

The knot in Heather's stomach tightened. She wasn't all that surprised to hear that Marco had been in on it, but she was shocked and disappointed to hear that Josh had participated in something so underhand.

"Aren't you going to say anything?" Violet demanded.

Heather furrowed her brow. "It's disheartening but understandable, to some extent. They're scared, Violet.

Someone's threatening them, trying to kill them, even going after their families. And the card they got in the mail alleges I'm a killer. Of course they're going to have questions. Fear makes people act in strange ways."

"And you're okay with that? That your friends are ganging up on you behind your back?" Violet shook her head in disbelief. "It's partly your own fault, you know. You could have made more of an effort to be sociable and keep in touch with them all these years. Reagan brought that up too. Why did you have to cut everyone off your senior year? And don't tell me it's because of what happened to me. I don't understand why you can't move on from that. It's almost as if you were the one it happened to. It's over. I've put it behind me. I have a husband and I'm about to become a mother. It's about time you moved on too."

"It's not like I haven't tried," Heather protested.

"Then try harder!"

"It's not that simple, Violet."

"Yes, it is. It's a choice. You choose to keep on hating. I chose to let it go. The man who attacked me is dead—"

"Yes he is! And I killed him!"

20

After a beat of silence, Violet spoke up, her tone considerably more gentle, "I'm sorry, Heather. I didn't mean to upset you. You have to stop with the guilt trip. We all wished him dead—"

"I didn't just wish him dead," Heather retorted. She got to her feet and began to pace in front of her sister. "I drove him to his death."

Violet gripped the back of her chair, looking up at her with a bewildered expression. "You're scaring me with your rambling." She gestured to the seat next to her. "Please, sit back down and let's talk about it. I know it was hard for you to get past the attack—you were always my protector. I get it, truly I do."

"No, you don't get it at all." Heather sank down opposite Violet and looked intently at her. "I'm going to tell you the truth about what happened that night. I was hoping it wouldn't come to this, but with everything that's going on, I feel I don't have a choice. Otherwise nothing's going to make sense to you, and I don't want to have to lie to you. The truth is, I killed Damien Kinney and I think someone knows."

Violet blinked in confusion and shook her head vehemently. "No you didn't. You're not making any sense, Heather. He crashed his truck into a tree. We read about it in the paper, remember?"

"I know he crashed into a tree," Heather said quietly. "I saw what happened because I was following him that night. He was trying to get away from me and he lost control of his truck."

Violet made a strange gulping sound at the back of her throat. "Why ... why didn't you ever tell me this before?"

"I couldn't risk anyone finding out, and I didn't want you to have the burden of keeping my secret. That's what the message in the card is about: *Heather has killed before. She'll do it again.*"

Violet took a shallow breath. "Following him doesn't make you a killer. He had alcohol in his system. He was over the legal limit. Drugs too. The autopsy ..." Her voice trailed off.

Heather nodded, dropping her head into her hands. "I know, but there's more to the story."

"What are you talking about?" Violet squeezed her hands together. "What did you do, Heather? Did you give him the drugs? Please, just tell me!"

Heather straightened up, chewing on her lip. "No, nothing like that. I was following him because I wanted to find out where he lived. I don't honestly know what I was planning to do when I caught up with him. I brought one of dad's shotguns in the car. I told myself it was only for protection, or maybe to threaten Damien with—to make him apologize for what he'd done to you. I wanted him to know what it felt like to feel powerless." She chewed on her nail, frowning. "But I never got the opportunity. He realized he was being followed and he blocked the road with his truck. He climbed out and started hammering on my car and kicking the door. So I held the gun up to the window. I think he recognized me then. He ran back to his truck and took off again, driving even more erratically than before. And then ... and then he hit the tree."

Heather fell silent for a moment.

"Don't stop now," Violet prompted her. "You have to finish. I need to know what you did."

"After he wrecked, I waited in my car for a few minutes. I was scared to get out in case he was waiting for me. When I finally plucked up the courage, I took the gun with me." A small sob escaped her lips.

Violet laid a hand on her arm. "But you didn't shoot him. He died from the injuries he sustained in the crash."

"That's the thing," Heather said softly. "He wasn't dead. I thought he was at first but then he lifted his head and stared at me. He pressed his fingers against the glass." Heather gave a barely perceptible shake of her head. "The look in his eyes was sheer desperation. He was pleading with me to help him. But I turned and walked away. I got back in my car and drove home and never reported the accident. I left him to die."

Violet tented her fingers over her mouth and nose, her eyes bulging as she stared at Heather. After a moment or two, she stammered, "But someone found him later that night."

"Not until four in the morning. He was dead by then. I could have saved him, but I didn't. I wanted him to die," Heather rasped.

Violet shook her head slowly, her face bleached of color. "I ... don't know what to say. I mean, I understand you felt you'd failed to protect me but—" Her voice faded away.

"I've had to live with what I did," Heather said softly. "I

chose revenge—I convinced myself back then it was justice. It cost me everything. I've lived with the guilt clinging to me like a leech all these years. And now what I did has come back to haunt me. My friends are being targeted because of me."

Violet wrinkled her brow. "You don't know that. It might not be connected to what's happening."

"I didn't want to believe it either, at first, but everything's pointing in that direction. That card: *Heather has killed before. She'll do it again.* Someone knows what I did." Heather interlocked her fingers and squeezed her hands together. "And it goes much deeper than that. I'm convinced Lindsay's death is somehow related to all of this."

"You're reading too much into it," Violet said. "Just because Lindsay was part of the student council, it doesn't mean her accident had anything to do with the threatening messages."

Heather picked at her nail. "I'm not convinced it was an accident." She got to her feet. "There's something I have to show you."

"Where are you going?"

"I need to get something. I'll be right back."

Minutes later, she returned to the kitchen with the hook she'd found in the brush and placed it on the table. "I found this not far from where Lindsay's body was discovered."

Violet picked it up and examined it. "What is it?"

"I don't know. A hook, obviously, but it looks as if it screws into a pole or something. Someone could have used this to cause the accident. Lindsay was an experienced off-road cyclist. It never made sense to me that she supposedly spun out on a little mud. What if someone hooked the wheel of her bike and deliberately caused her to wreck?"

Violet dropped the hook on the table and jerked her

hand away from it as though it had taken on a macabre aura as an instrument of death. "That ... would be murder."

"Exactly," Heather replied. "And if this person has killed before, they will kill again."

"But why kill Lindsay if it's you they're after?" Violet asked.

Heather gave a helpless shrug. "Perhaps they thought my friends knew what I did and covered it up. Or maybe they're simply trying to punish me any way they can, by hurting the people I'm closest to."

Violet shot her a nervous look. "So the note that came here: *You should be afraid,* was a warning for me. I might be next."

Heather wrapped her arms around Violet and hugged her tight. "I'm not going to let anything happen to you, or your baby. I'll get to the bottom of this, I promise you."

Her phone vibrated in her pocket. "It's Steve," she said, flicking a finger across the screen to take the call. "Hey, how's Sydney doing?"

"Better, thanks," he replied. "She wants to see you."

"O-kay," Heather said tentatively. "It's almost ten o'clock. How about I stop by the hospital first thing in the morning?"

"She wants to speak with you now. She says it's important."

Heather rubbed a hand across her brow. "All right. Tell her I'm on my way." She hung up and turned to Violet. "I'm going back to the hospital. Sydney wants to talk to me about something. Don't wait up for me."

TWENTY MINUTES LATER, Heather stepped into Sydney's hospital room for the second time that day. Steve was stretched out in a recliner chair next to the bed. His eyes shot open at the sound of her footsteps. "Thanks for coming," he said, getting to his feet. "Syd insisted it couldn't wait until morning." He bent over the bed and shook her gently awake. "Honey, Heather's here."

Sydney's eyes fluttered open and latched onto Heather.

"How are you feeling?" Heather asked.

Sydney swallowed a few breaths before answering, "My throat hurts. They pumped my stomach." She gestured for Heather to come closer. "Sorry, I have to whisper."

"Don't worry about it. I'm just glad you're okay," Heather said.

Sydney attempted a weak smile. "I feel bad now for blaming the oysters. You heard they found ethylene glycol in my system?"

Heather gave a somber nod. "The police are trying to find out how it was administered to you."

"I've been trying to figure that out too." Sydney let out a moan as she attempted to sit up. Steve immediately leapt to his feet to adjust her pillows.

"The police questioned everyone at the coffee shop, and Steve, of course," Sydney went on. "They didn't get anywhere. But this evening when I woke up, I remembered something that happened. I'd just taken the lid off my latte to add some sugar when my phone rang. I stepped outside the coffee shop to take the call, and this woman bumped up against me—sent my coffee flying." Sydney paused and rumpled her brow as if visualizing the scene. "She was very flustered and insisted on buying me another drink. A couple of minutes later, she came back out and handed me my latte and apologized again profusely. I didn't think anything of it at the time, but now I'm wondering if she tampered with my drink."

Heather exchanged a loaded look with Steve. "Did you tell the police about this woman?"

"Not yet," he replied. "Syd wanted to get your take on it first."

Heather tented her fingers in front of her, deep in thought. It made sense to her that a woman was behind what was happening. The vengeful notes and the flowers weren't something a man would naturally gravitate toward. "What did this woman look like?"

"She had long, brown hair in a thick braid. I'm guessing she was around our age. She was wearing tinted glasses— you know those weird orange lenses for light sensitivity—so I couldn't see her eyes very well."

"Do you remember anything else about her? Any distinguishing characteristics?"

Sydney traced her fingers across her brow. "Her voice was kind of low-pitched. To be honest, I was distracted trying to wipe foam off my shoes and answer my phone."

"The coffee shop might have a camera system," Steve chipped in.

Heather nodded. "I'll check in the morning. In the meantime, you need to call the police and let them know what you told me. It's important they find that woman as soon as possible."

"So you think it's the same person?" Sydney asked in a hushed tone. "The one who's behind everything that's been going on?"

"Possibly, or she could be a hired gun doing someone else's dirty work," Heather replied. "Either way, we need to locate her."

Sydney nodded, her eyes drifting closed as she leaned back against her pillows.

"I should get going and let her sleep," Heather said, nodding goodbye to Steve.

"Thanks for coming," he answered. "She wouldn't rest until I called you."

"Let me know how she's doing in the morning," Heather said, before exiting the room.

To her surprise, Violet was still sitting at the kitchen table when she got home.

"Don't get mad at me," Violet said, raising her hands in an apologetic gesture. "I couldn't sleep. Now that I'm involved, I want to know what's going on every step of the way. How's Sydney doing?"

Heather retrieved a bottle of water from the refrigerator and joined her sister at the table. "Better. She remembered something strange that happened this morning." Heather unscrewed the cap on her water and took a long sip before continuing, "Sydney was on the phone outside the coffee shop when a woman bumped into her and spilled her drink. She insisted on buying her a new one, and brought it out to her while Sydney was still on the phone." Heather blew out a heavy breath. "It was the only opportunity anyone had to poison her that morning."

"Do you think Sydney could identify the woman if she saw her again?" Violet asked.

"Probably. She got a good, up-close look at her. She said she had long brown hair in a thick braid and was wearing tinted glasses."

Violet's face paled. "That's the same description the florist gave me of the woman who ordered the forget-me-nots."

"What?" Heather gasped. "You never mentioned anything about a braid."

"I said brown hair and glasses—" Violet broke off. "I forgot about the braid. I'm sorry—I'm not good at details. I'm not the PI, am I?"

Heather flapped a hand at her, her thoughts racing. "It doesn't matter. The important thing is that we know for sure there's a connection now."

"What are you going to do about it?" Violet asked.

Heather reached for the hook lying on the table and twisted it thoughtfully between her fingers. "Find out who this woman is and stop her before she kills again."

21

Early the following morning, Heather slid into a vinyl booth opposite Josh in Rosie's Diner.

"Thanks for coming. I hope you're hungry," Josh said, handing her a laminated menu. "This place is all about a hearty breakfast."

Heather twisted her lips. "I mostly need coffee—I didn't sleep much."

Josh raised a quizzical brow, and she took a few minutes to bring him up to speed on everything Sydney had told her the previous night.

Right on cue, their waitress appeared with a pot of coffee in one fist and two mugs in the other. "Ready to order?" She slapped the mugs down on the table and proceeded to fill them.

"You're reading my mind," Heather said to her. "Poached eggs and toast for me, please."

"I'll have the country omelet, and a water," Josh added.

After filling their mugs to the brim, the waitress swooped up their menus before shuffling off again.

"I'm sure you're wondering why I wanted to talk to you alone," Josh said.

Heather sipped her coffee. "Your text was pretty vague. I assume you want more details about my visit with Dan Wilcox—I couldn't say too much in front of the others."

Josh's forehead creased. "Actually, I wanted to talk to you about something else. I've been agonizing over whether or not to tell you, but it doesn't feel right to keep you in the dark, especially after what happened to Sydney."

Heather angled a brow at him. "Now I'm intrigued."

Josh took a swig of coffee, his face beset with worry. "Reagan suspects you might be behind everything that's going on, including Sydney's poisoning. You know she called your sister, right? She blindsided us with that after insisting on meeting with me and Marco."

Heather nodded. "Violet's fuming about that."

"Reagan's got this bee in her bonnet that you're still holding a grudge against us—her, in particular. She's pegged you as some kind of unhinged vigilante for justice. I'm not sure Marco entirely buys it, but she's got him thinking too. He reckons it's fishy that you and Sydney ate at the same restaurant last night."

Heather fought to keep her expression blank, her heart thundering in her chest. *A vigilante for justice* hit a little too close to home. She laced her fingers around her coffee mug and peered at Josh over the rim. "What about you? Are you worried I might be a psycho PI bent on avenging my high school nemesis?"

Josh gave a sheepish grin. "It wasn't my first thought when I saw you again. But, as you can imagine, it puts me in a difficult position—Reagan wanting us to meet behind your back and all. She's looking into hiring a PI to follow you around and see what you're really up to."

Heather laughed. "Go for it. I guarantee you I can shake any tail you put on me."

"I don't doubt it," Josh responded, as the waitress arrived with their food. She slapped their plates down and fished a straw out of her apron pocket for Josh's water. "Anything else I can get you two?"

"I think that's it," Heather replied. "Looks great, thanks." She reached for the salt and pepper and doused her eggs.

"I can't believe you're not more upset about Reagan's allegations," Josh remarked.

Heather sipped her coffee thoughtfully. "To tell you the truth, I'm wondering if she's trying to deflect attention from herself. Did you know that she and Marco had a fling years ago?"

Josh hefted his brows upward. "Funny, I always suspected there was something those two were hiding. How did you find out?"

"Reagan told me. She was worried Roy might have found out about it and set the fire at Bella Calabria to punish them. Supposedly, he's furious that Reagan got custody of Lucy. I talked to Marco about it too. He backed up her story. They don't think Anna knows, but she does. She thinks they have a *deeper connection*, as she put it, than they're letting on—whatever that's supposed to mean."

Josh frowned. "Maybe she thinks they're still carrying on behind her back."

Heather chewed on a piece of poached egg and swallowed. She didn't want to share her suspicion, yet, that Lucy was Marco's daughter—not until she'd done some more digging. "I don't think that's it. Whatever went on between Reagan and Marco is over. But Anna got me thinking. I've been wondering if Reagan invested in his business or something. If the business is in trouble, and she wants her money back out, the arson might have been an attempt to defraud the insurance company—Marco and Reagan could have schemed together. Maybe that's the connection Anna was alluding to."

"Judging by the way Marco throws money around, I don't think he's struggling," Josh said, reaching for the ketchup. "I wouldn't put too much stock in Anna's speculations. Sounds like she's nursing a lot of hurt about the affair. Unfortunately, those wounds won't heal until she confronts Marco about it." He hesitated, and then added, "Speaking of healing, you said you don't think Dan Wilcox is coping well."

Heather set down her fork and looked at Josh with an air of compassion. "I'm not going to lie to you, if he doesn't make some changes soon, he's going to end up destroying his life."

Josh scrubbed a hand over his chin. "I blame myself for the situation he's in."

Heather pushed a piece of egg around on her plate, mopping up the yolk. "This is the point where I'm supposed to say you shouldn't blame yourself, but I get it," she said, in a wistful tone. "It's hard not to wish you could go back and do things differently."

Josh threw her a curious look. "What would you do differently?"

Heather faked a smile. "Nothing. I'm just rambling. Changing the subject, do you mind if I give Sydney a quick call? I need to find out if the police tracked down any camera footage of the woman in the coffee shop."

"Go right ahead," Josh said, digging back into his omelet.

Heather dialed the number and waited, relieved when Sydney answered the phone herself. "Hey, Syd! How are you feeling?"

"Weak, but better than yesterday. I'm ready to go home as soon as they discharge me."

"Have the police been in touch this morning?" Heather asked.

"One of the detectives stopped by a few minutes ago. He wanted to know if I could recall any more details about the woman. I guess the coffee shop doesn't have any cameras."

Heather grimaced and pressed the phone to her cheek. Without any footage, their hopes of identifying the stranger were greatly diminished.

"Hang on a minute, Heather," Sydney said. "Steve just walked in." There was a scuffling sound and then a hushed conversation before Steve came on the line. "Sydney needs to rest now." He abruptly hung up before Heather had a chance to respond.

"Everything all right?" Josh asked, picking up on her perturbed expression.

She exhaled a breath. "I think Reagan's been spreading her poison. I'm pretty sure she shared her suspicions about me with Steve. He wasn't too happy to catch me talking to Sydney. He more or less told me not to bother her anymore."

"Perhaps I shouldn't have told you what Reagan said." Josh's eyes crinkled with concern. "It's going to be tough pretending you don't know she was talking about you behind your back. If you want to skip lunch with Reagan and Marco, I can tell them you're following up on leads or something."

Heather shook her head. "No, that only opens me up to more suspicion. I need to confront them about the call they made to Violet. Reagan's up to something. I just hope for her sake it doesn't have anything to do with Lindsay's death."

Josh flashed her a startled look. "Lindsay's death? What do you mean?"

"Uh, I meant to say, with what's happened *since* Lindsay's death." Heather pressed her napkin to her lips and pushed her plate to one side. She had slipped up. She couldn't bring up the matter of the hook or her suspicion that Lindsay had been murdered. Until she could back it up with some evidence, it sounded like a far-fetched theory, and the last thing she wanted to do was add to the picture Reagan was painting of her as an *unhinged vigilante*.

The expression on Josh's face cleared. He signaled to the waitress for the check. "What are your plans for this morning?"

"I'm going to swing by Roy's house and see if he's home. One of these days we're bound to connect."

"I'd offer to go with you, but I have a client appointment this morning," Josh said, getting to his feet.

"No worries. I do my best surveillance work alone," Heather assured him.

WHEN SHE PULLED up outside Roy's house, a dark blue Toyota Tacoma truck was parked in the driveway. Finally, she had timed it right. She rang the doorbell and waited for someone to answer. After a few minutes, the front door opened and Aidy stared out at her. "Oh, it's you again."

"I'm looking for Roy. Is that his truck in the driveway?"

"No, it's my brother's." Aidy folded her arms in front of her. "Roy isn't here. I told him someone stopped by about an inheritance and he got all freaked out about it and took off. Haven't seen him since last night. He wanted to know what you looked like. I think he thought you were going to serve him papers or something." She leaned casually against the door post. "Is that what you're really up to?"

Heather stretched a polite smile across her face. "I'm afraid Bodensteiner and Kern is not at liberty to discuss a client's business with a third party."

Aidy's lips curled into a peevish smile. "So that's what I am now. The third party."

"Just let Roy know I need to talk to him as soon as possible," Heather said. "And no, I'm not here to serve him. I can assure you he's not in any kind of trouble."

"Not with you, he's not," Aidy called after her as Heather crossed the street to her car.

She was about to drive off when she noticed a text from Lindsay's mom, Pam Robinson.

Heather, dear, I'm coming home today. If you're still in town I'd love to see you. Any time tomorrow would be fine.

Heather quickly typed out a response confirming that she would stop by around ten the following morning. She was eager to talk to Pam about Lindsay's close friends and acquaintances and try and piece together any information that might shed some light on what had happened to her. She would have to take care not to say anything to alarm her. The last thing she wanted was a grieving Pam worrying about whether her daughter had been murdered.

Shortly before noon, Heather arrived at The Sardinian where she'd arranged to meet the others for lunch. She braced herself for an uncomfortable meeting as she headed inside. There was no point in beating around the bush. She had to address the underhanded phone call to her sister head-on. The atmosphere was tense as she pulled out a chair and took a seat at the table. Josh gave her a tight smile and a subtle nod as if to say that everything would be all right, which, of course, it wouldn't. Things were about to get ugly.

Heather fixed a penetrating gaze on Reagan. "Violet told me you called her."

Reagan's eyes narrowed. "I was concerned about you."

"Is that what you call making wild allegations and terrifying my sister? I thought you would have been more mature than that by now."

"Hey! Take it easy you two," Marco cut in, "We're not here to argue. We're all just trying to figure this mess out."

"Are we?" Heather retorted. "It seems I was brought back to Iowa under false pretenses. All of a sudden, I've gone from investigator to suspect."

"Oh stop acting like we're back in high school!" Reagan chided. "You were always so easily offended."

"Back in high school?" Heather echoed. "Like when you started spreading rumors about me?"

"See what I mean?" Reagan huffed, turning to Marco and Josh.

"Look, this is getting us nowhere," Josh said. "We have a real suspect now. We need to talk about how we're going to track down the woman in the coffee shop."

"It might be easier than we thought. PI's are masters of disguise," Reagan said, arching an accusing brow. "*Once a killer, always a killer.* Isn't that what the note said? What does that mean, Heather? Did you kill someone?"

22

Heather woke the following morning with a pounding headache. She had stormed out of The Sardinian at lunch the previous day leaving Reagan, Marco, and Josh with jaws agape after telling them in no uncertain terms that she would proceed with the investigation alone. Despite Marco and Josh advocating on Heather's behalf, Reagan had refused to back down on her accusations. It was a complete turnaround from a couple of days earlier when Reagan had been convinced that Roy was behind everything. Something had changed in the intervening days. Had she spoken to him? And where was Roy? Aidy claimed she hadn't seen him in over twenty-four hours. Was she covering for him?

With a reluctant groan, Heather flung back the covers and climbed out of bed. She needed to locate Roy and get to the bottom of his involvement in all of this, and she wasn't going to find him by sleeping.

"Feeling better?" Violet asked when she joined her in the kitchen.

"Caffeine will help," Heather said, as she padded over to

the coffeemaker and poured herself a cup. "I just can't figure out what Reagan's game is—why she's trying to pin everything on me. She's completely changed her tune from a few days ago."

"It's because of the latest message—that you've killed before and you'll do it again," Violet said. "You have to admit, it sounds pretty ominous."

Heather sipped her coffee. "Josh and Marco aren't taking it seriously."

"What about Sydney?"

"Steve's essentially cut off any communication with her," Heather answered. "Reagan's convinced him I'm not to be trusted. I can't really blame him. He doesn't know me from Adam—he's only trying to protect his wife. Let's face it, somebody poisoned her."

Violet shivered, her hands instinctively hugging her belly.

Heather drained the rest of her coffee and got to her feet. "I need to jump in the shower. I'm going to visit Pam this morning."

"I didn't know she was back in town," Violet remarked.

"Her sister and brother-in-law drove her down yesterday. She wants me to stop by to see her. I have a feeling I could be there a while—she might need help sorting through Lindsay's things. It's going to be very emotional for her."

Violet threw her an anxious look. "Do you want me to come with you? It won't be easy for you either, looking through old high school yearbook photos and the like."

Heather gave a nod of acknowledgement. "I know, but I need to talk to Pam alone. I have to find out who Lindsay was hanging out with in the months before her death."

"So you still think there's a connection between her accident and the threats?" Violet asked.

"Let's put it this way," Heather replied. "I need to rule out that possibility."

"I'll make you some breakfast before you go," Violet said, getting to her feet. "How about blueberry pancakes? I know they're your favorite."

Heather tweaked a smile. "Lindsay got me hooked. She made the best blueberry pancakes."

"I can't believe you never came back to see her all these years," Violet said, readying her griddle and pancake batter. "Why did you let your relationship with her slide?"

Heather traced her finger around the rim of her coffee mug. "It's complicated. Lindsay was the only person I ever told what I did that night. I think the secret became like a ball and chain for her. Instead of getting easier to bear over time, it only got harder. She wanted me to drive back out there that night to check on Damien, or at least place an anonymous call to the police. I think she was shocked at what I'd done. She still loved me as a friend, but she looked at me differently after that. She came out to see me in LA a couple of times, but she didn't care for the place."

Violet set a plate of blueberry pancakes in front of Heather. The tantalizing aroma of warm blueberries and syrup filled her nostrils bringing back memories of lazy Saturday mornings spent at Lindsay's house. Heather set her lips in a determined line. She had failed her as a friend all these years. She owed it to her, and to Pam, to find out what had really happened, no matter how long it took. She couldn't go through the rest of her life wondering if Lindsay's death had been an accident, or something more insidious.

"I have to admit you make some pretty awesome pancakes, Vivi," Heather said, lifting her plate when she was done and carrying it over to the sink. "You'll be a great mom."

Violet let out a snort of laughter. "I only know how to make pancakes and scrambled eggs. My kid's destined to be malnourished."

Heather rinsed her dishes and loaded them into the dishwasher. "I can't cook to save my life either. Not that I ever practice. By the way, don't include me in your dinner plans tonight. I'll probably end up taking Pam out to eat, and I want to do a little more surveillance at Roy's house afterward. Do you mind if I share your good news with Pam? I know she'll be happy for you."

Violet grinned. "Of course. Just ask her to keep it to herself for now."

SHORTLY BEFORE 10:00 A.M., Heather pulled up outside Pam's house. The place was smaller than she remembered, and it looked like it could use a coat of paint and some TLC. The lawn had been kept up, but the lush beds of roses that Heather recalled from bygone years had been replaced by more practical, low-maintenance shrubs. She rang the doorbell and stepped back to wait. Just as she was about to try knocking, she heard a faint voice, "Coming, dear."

When the door scraped open, Heather fought to hide her shock. The shrunken woman on the walker in front of her looked nothing like Lindsay's sprightly mother from years ago. Pam had lost a lot of weight and her face had fallen with age—partly from grief, no doubt.

"Heather! How lovely to see you again. Come on in." She turned awkwardly in the hallway and led the way at a painstakingly slow pace back to the kitchen. "My sister and brother-in-law left a couple of hours ago to drive back to Sioux City."

"How was your time with them?" Heather asked.

"I suppose it did me some good to get away for a few weeks—change of scene and all that. But to tell you the truth, I was glad to get home again. I can't run from reality forever," Pam replied, maneuvering her walker through the door leading into the kitchen.

"It looks great in here," Heather said. "When did you remodel the kitchen?"

"Five years ago. Lindsay kept bugging me to do it." A momentary flicker of sadness crossed Pam's face before she smiled at Heather. "You know how she was when she got a notion in her head about something."

Heather gave a nod of agreement. "Only too well." She eased Pam into a chair and then sat down next to her. "I still can't believe she's gone."

Pam's eyes glistened with the threat of tears. "Just this morning, I woke up and thought to myself, I'd better call Lindsay and let her know I got back safely from my sister's." She shook her head sadly. "I always told her she raced those bikes far too fast."

"Is that what the police think?" Heather asked. "That she was racing?"

Pam raised her liver-spotted hands in a gesture of helplessness. "They don't know, do they? It's impossible to say how fast she was going. But you know how hard she pushed herself. She was always training for one race or another. Such a tragic accident." Pam blinked earnestly at Heather.

"So ... shocking," Heather mumbled. Sowing seeds of doubt in Pam's mind that it had been an accident would be cruel, without the evidence to back it up.

"It was such bad luck that she knocked herself out on

that rock," Pam went on, with a weary sigh. "She was completely vulnerable at that point. Animal control said there was probably a breeding pair of rattlesnakes nearby. She was bitten twice you know."

Heather shook her head. "I can't even imagine how horrific it must have been for her—and for you."

"Identifying her body was the hardest thing I've ever had to do in my life," Pam acknowledged. "The only comfort I have is believing she was unconscious when she was bitten and didn't suffer."

Heather reached for Pam's hand and squeezed it. "I'm sure you're right."

Pam pulled a tissue from her sleeve and wiped her nose. "How about some coffee?"

"Let me make it," Heather said, getting to her feet. "You'll have to give me directions around this new kitchen of yours."

She returned to the table a few minutes later with two steaming mugs of coffee.

"Would you like a muffin to go with that?" Pam asked. "I made my sour cream and cherry recipe."

"I might take you up on that later. I had a big breakfast of blueberry pancakes at Violet's house."

Pam's face brightened. "How is your sister?"

"She's doing great—she's pregnant. She just found out so keep it to yourself for now."

Pam clapped her hands together. "Oh, that is wonderful news. I know she's been trying for a long time. I'm so happy for her. When's the baby due?"

Heather furrowed her brow. "Sometime in March. I forget the exact date."

Pam reached for her coffee mug. "So, tell me about your

life in LA. Lindsay said you're a private investigator to the stars. That sounds exciting."

Heather laughed. "It's not like the movies. I'm mostly hired to surveil cheating spouses for divorce cases."

"Do you have enough work to keep you busy?" Pam asked.

"More than I can handle," Heather said, with a wry grin. "I won't run out of work in LA."

Pam rubbed her hip and glanced over at the kitchen counter. "Do you mind fetching me that Ibuprofen by the toaster please?"

Heather retrieved the bottle and handed it to her. "How long have you been using the walker?"

"Six months or so. I need a hip replacement but without Lindsay here to help me recover, it's going to be a lot more difficult. I can't even lift down the tubs in her old room that I want to go through."

"I can help you with that," Heather said. "I'm available today for whatever you need."

"That's kind of you, dear. It would be nice to look through some photos together."

Stepping into Lindsay's old room was more painful than Heather had anticipated. Unlike the kitchen, Lindsay's bedroom was virtually unchanged from when they'd been in high school—the same bed and dresser, the furry beanbag chair they had shared so many conversations in, even the lava lamp they had picked out together at a local flea market. Heather swallowed the lump in her throat, a slew of memories stirring up the depths of her grief.

Steeling herself for the task at hand, she made her way over to the closet and began lifting down the plastic containers on the shelf above the clothing rod. She made several trips back-and-forth to the kitchen and then sat down with Pam to go through the tubs.

"Can you believe I kept all her artwork from Kindergarten?" Pam exclaimed. "This stick figure's supposed to be me. She made this for Mother's Day. Listen to this: *my mom is six inches tall and her favorite food is mushrooms and chicken nuggets. When I go to school she likes to go shopping and collect shells.*" Pam chuckled as she folded the sheet back up and set it aside. "That's a keeper."

"Here are her high school graduation photos," Heather said, leafing through the pictures. "I can't believe we thought we looked cool back then. Such goofy hairdos." She passed the photos to Pam.

"I think you both look beautiful, so young and full of promise," Pam gushed.

Heather reached for another envelope and slid the contents out. Her blood ran cold. It was a photo of Lindsay, leaning up to kiss the cheek of a much older man outside the car wash where she'd worked.

23

Heather hurriedly stuffed the incriminating photo back into the envelope and slipped it into her pocket while Pam was engrossed in the graduation pictures. She didn't know anything about Lindsay's affair—and Heather meant to keep it that way. The photo would only trigger some uncomfortable questions in the grieving woman's mind.

Heather had never met Lindsay's boss, Bill, or even seen a picture of him before. Lindsay had been very secretive about their relationship, insisting Bill didn't want her friends knowing about him until he'd divorced his wife. But then he had upped and disappeared overnight, leaving Lindsay in the lurch. Heather couldn't help wondering if he'd gotten in touch with Lindsay again.

She spent the rest of the day assisting Pam with various tasks around the house. The bulk of their time was dedicated to sifting through Lindsay's personal possessions, an arduous process filled with tears and countless tea breaks— deciding what to keep, what to donate, and what to throw out. Pam insisted that Heather take Lindsay's old jewelry box, along with a couple of photo albums from their high school days. By six o'clock that evening, Heather's car was stacked full of clothes and miscellaneous items that she'd offered to drop off at one of the local thrift stores.

"How about I take you out to dinner, Pam," she suggested. "I'm sure you don't feel like cooking after working all day."

"To tell you the truth, dear, I'm exhausted. Another time perhaps. Thank you so much for your help today. I honestly don't know how I would have got it all done without you."

"Don't hesitate to call or text if you need anything else. I'll be around for the next few weeks or so," Heather said, as she gave her a hug in parting.

On the way back to Violet's place, she stopped at a pizzeria to satisfy her growling stomach. She ordered a medium pepperoni and sat down at a table in the back with her laptop. If someone had found out what she'd done, then she needed to go back to the beginning to figure out who it could be. She would start by digging up the old newspaper articles on Damien's accident. After opening up her browser, she ran multiple searches on the story. The reporting was all very cut and dried. No suggestion of foul play, no mention of another vehicle on the road that night. By all accounts, it had simply been another tragic DUI death. There had been no investigation beyond the autopsy and toxicology reports.

She pulled up the police report on the accident, but it contained no information other than what she already knew. Without witnesses to interview, there was little for the police to investigate. After scrolling through some additional search results, she happened upon a newspaper article that mentioned the funeral. She clicked on it and studied the photo of a beaming Damien with his family. All at once, her skin began to crawl with a foreboding feeling.

She enlarged the black-and-white picture and stared at it in disbelief. Kitted out in his football uniform, with a football tucked beneath his arm, Damien stood proudly between a smartly dressed man and woman. The text below the photo read: *William and Judy Kinney pictured with their son, Damien.*

With shaking fingers, Heather pulled out the photo of Lindsay and Bill that was burning a hole in her pocket and compared it. There was no doubt that she was looking at the same man. William Kinney was Damien's father. The pizza churned in her stomach. Her instincts had been right all along. This was the connection she had been searching for —the missing link between Damien, Lindsay's death, the arson, the threatening messages, and everything else that had been happening since the reunion. Heather's brain pounded against her skull as the shocking realization hit her like a thunderbolt. Lindsay must have told Bill that Heather had left Damien for dead. And now he was out for revenge.

Heather stared transfixed into the eyes of Damien Kinney's father as he smiled back at her. He was coming for her, and anyone close to her. The thought that he might have orchestrated Lindsay's death because she'd covered up what happened to his son chilled her soul. There wasn't a minute to waste—she had to find him before he struck again.

With trembling fingers, she got to work researching carwash operations in Davenport. She couldn't remember the name of the one Lindsay had worked at, but it had been an upscale hand-wash-and-detail operation. With painstaking focus, she pulled up the details on every car wash business in existence in Davenport twenty years ago and drilled down to the information on the owners. She had just swallowed a bite of pizza when she got a hit. The food stuck in her throat. William Kinney, forty-one years old, owner and proprietor of Elite Finish. Heather quickly logged into one of the proprietary databases she subscribed to, added William Kinney's details to the search form, and submitted it. Moments later, a photo popped up on her screen. A chill skittered down her spine. It was Lindsay's Bill all right. A good-looking man in an arrogant sort of way—his expression not unlike his son's.

Heather leaned back in her chair and dragged a hand through her hair. Finally a breakthrough. Now to nail down Bill's current contact details. Lindsay had maintained she had no idea where he had gone after he bailed out on her. It was possible he was living out of state. If it took getting on an airplane to find him, then that's what Heather would do. She pushed her plate aside and set about the task of finding out where William Kinney was living at present. Minutes later, her search came to an abrupt halt. She stared at the screen in disbelief, her fingers curling into a fist of frustration. William Kinney was deceased. He had passed away from pancreatic cancer six months earlier. Heather reread the information, dumbstruck. Bill Kinney had turned out to be a dead end. She had no choice but to go back to the drawing board.

She reached for another slice of pizza and munched on it mindlessly, washing it down with her Diet Coke as she tried to reassemble her fragmented thoughts. Bill Kinney had died before the class reunion took place. That still left the possibility that Bill's ex-wife, Judy—Damien's mother—was somehow involved. After all, it had been a woman who had placed the forget-me-not order and sent Sydney's drink flying outside the coffee shop. Granted, Judy Kinney's hair was short in the photo, but it had been taken twenty years earlier. She could have grown it out since, or she might have been wearing a wig with a braid. The more pressing question was why she had waited until now to avenge her son's death. Perhaps Bill had only told her in the months before his death—wanting to get it off his chest as dying people do.

Heather scrubbed her hands over her face. Her head was pounding, and her thoughts were growing choppier by the minute. She needed to talk this over with someone in a logical manner, get another perspective. After a moment's hesitation, she pulled out her phone and texted Josh. He had unmasked Reagan's duplicity—she hoped she was right that she could trust him.

The server stopped at her table and reached for her empty plate. "Can I get you anything else?" he asked, his tone verging on snippy.

"I'll take a refill on the Diet Coke, please." Heather flashed him an apologetic smile. She could tell by his expression that the pizzeria was getting ready to close, but she needed a few more minutes to locate a current address for Judy Kinney—if she even went by Kinney anymore. She could have reverted to her maiden name after her divorce, or she might have remarried. After another twenty minutes of research, Heather finally had the information she needed in hand. Damien's mother was living in Davenport in a one-bedroom condo. Marital status: *divorced*.

Heather packed up her laptop and left a generous tip on the table, before making her way out to her car. She had planned on driving by Roy's house again this evening, but he was no longer a priority. The investigation had taken an abrupt change of course. Instead, she would pay Judy Kinney a visit. She wasn't sure what the best approach to take would be. Perhaps she should stick with some version of the truth and introduce herself as Lindsay's best friend. She could say she was trying to track down Bill to return some belongings of his—play dumb to the fact that he was dead. Alternatively, she could admit to being a private investigator hired by Lindsay's friends to look into her death, and watch Judy's reaction. Either way, it was too late to knock on the woman's door tonight. She would have to content herself with driving by her condo and scoping out the situation.

Heather had just put the car into gear when her phone rang. She didn't recognize the number, but it was a local area code. "Hello," she said, waiting for the person on the other end of the line to identify themselves.

"Is this ... Heather Nelson?"

"Speaking," Heather replied.

"It's Aidy. You know ... the third party." Her attempt at humor fell apart—at odds with her agitated tone.

Heather frowned. This wasn't a distraction she needed right now. "Has Roy returned?"

"No. That's why I'm calling. He's ... he's dead."

24

"The police found Roy's body in his truck last night," Aidy went on to explain, her voice wavering. "His brother had reported him missing."

Heather gripped her phone tighter, her brain exploding from the dizzying news. Just when she'd zeroed in on the link between the threatening messages and Lindsay's death, a wrench had been thrown in her theory. Roy had turned up —dead. Did he have some connection to Damien's family? Or was Reagan's shady ex just muddying the water of her investigation? "Are they sure it's Roy?" she asked.

"Yes. He had his ID on him," Aidy answered. "The cops asked his brother to identify the body."

"I'm so sorry, Aidy," Heather blurted out, still trying to absorb the shock. Her mind was racing in myriad directions. Did this have anything at all to do with her investigation? Roy had been spooked when he heard someone was looking for him. But why? What did he have to hide? "Do the police know what happened?"

"Blunt force trauma to the head," Aidy replied. "They found his body in the bed of his truck. They don't think he was killed there though. They think someone dumped him there afterward."

Heather frowned. "Do you have any idea who would do something like this to him?"

"Not really. I mean, Roy fell out with enough people—me included." Aidy hesitated. "That spiel you gave me—*law offices of Bodensteiner and Kern*. It's bogus, isn't it? There is no inheritance. What did you actually want to talk to Roy about?"

Heather thought for a moment before responding. There was no need to pretend anymore now that Roy was dead. "I'm sorry I wasn't able to be more upfront with you the other day. It's a confidentiality thing. My name's Heather Nelson. I'm a private investigator. I was hired to look into something that Roy may or may not have been involved in."

"Is that why Roy was killed?"

Heather blew out a breath. "To be honest, I'm not entirely sure. The case I'm working on takes more twists and turns by the minute. As you said yourself, Roy made his fair share of enemies along the way, so his murder could be totally unrelated to my investigation. I'm not at liberty to say much more than that, but I'm sure the police will keep you posted on any developments."

"Yeah, right," Aidy said, sounding peeved. "I'm not family, remember? I only found out Roy was dead when his brother called me after the police came knocking on his door last night."

"I'm truly sorry," Heather said. "Will you have to move out of the house?"

Aidy let out a scathing laugh. "Not much point in waiting to be kicked out. Not that I have much stuff here anyway. Most of it's at my sister's place where I was living before."

"Look, I can't promise anything, but I'll do my best to dig around and see if I can shed some light on what happened to Roy," Heather said. "Keep me posted on your end if the police inquiry unearths anything."

"Yeah, sure," Aidy said in a tone that suggested she wouldn't put herself out to get in touch again.

Heather hung up and dropped her phone into the center console. Her breath baulked at a disturbing thought. Someone might have been watching her stalking Roy's house and killed him to stop him talking.

LATE THE FOLLOWING MORNING, Heather received a cryptic message from Marco.

I need to talk to you privately. Not at the restaurant. Can you meet me at Centennial Park at noon?

Heather frowned as she reread the message. What could Marco possibly want to talk to her about that he didn't want the others knowing? Another confession? Perhaps Josh was right, and the affair with Reagan had never ended. Heather felt sick to her stomach at the thought. Dave seemed like a genuinely nice man who deserved better, and, as for Anna, it was clear that she had been deeply hurt by Marco's betrayal, resigning herself to staying with him for the sake of the children.

See you at noon, Heather typed back, adding a thumbs up emoji. She checked the rest of her messages, disappointed to see there was still no response from Josh. Was he deliberately avoiding her?

· · ·

SHE SPOTTED Marco before he saw her. He was sitting on a bench by the river, hunched forward, elbows resting on his knees, deep in thought.

"Hey, you!" she called out to him as she drew closer.

He glanced up and flashed her an absent smile before reaching for a paper bag on the bench next to him. "Hope you like turkey. I brought sandwiches." He handed her one, along with a bottle of water. "Thanks for coming. I know we didn't part on the best of terms. Reagan was way out of line. I still want to help you with this investigation—whatever you need, it's yours."

Heather shrugged. "It's just business. I work better alone anyway. So, what did you want to talk to me about? Your message sounded urgent."

His dark eyes locked with hers. "Roy's dead."

Heather nodded slowly. "I heard. His girlfriend, Aidy, called me last night."

Marco frowned. "Did she say what happened?"

"Only that he was found in the bed of his truck and that there was evidence of blunt force trauma. How did you find out about it?"

He rubbed a hand over his dark stubble and glanced at a couple walking by with their poodle. "The police called me this morning."

"The police!" Heather arched a questioning brow. "Why did they call you?"

Marco swallowed and lowered his voice. "They found accelerant in Roy's truck—the same accelerant that was used in the arson. They wanted to know if I'd had any dealings with Roy in the past, so I had to tell them about the affair." He was quiet for a long moment and then added, "The thing is, I'm wondering now if Reagan planned the arson and talked Roy into doing her dirty work for her. You know how she kept pushing the idea that he was behind everything before she started on you. She might even have planted the accelerant in his truck after he was killed to make him look like the guilty party." He rubbed his hands over his face and groaned. "I can't believe this is happening. I should never have gotten involved with her."

"That's water under the bridge," Heather said. When Marco didn't respond, she asked, "It is over between you two, isn't it?"

He got to his feet and paced back and forth in front of her, his sandwich untouched. "I'm still living with the repercussions."

Heather held her breath, waiting for him to elaborate. He flopped back down on the bench and unscrewed the cap on his water bottle. "You haven't reacted yet to my theory about Reagan masterminding the arson. It's a pretty bold allegation." He narrowed his dark eyes and studied her. "You know she's still trying to convince me that you're behind everything—that you're unhinged."

Heather twisted her lips. "I'd have to be deranged to risk my career like that. Do I look like an arsonist or a poisoner to you?"

"Give me a break." Marco leaned back on the bench and stared up at the iron gray sky for a moment. "But I am worried Reagan had something to do with it. She's protesting too much, trying too hard to pin it on other people. First it was Roy, and then it was you, and now Roy turns up dead and, conveniently, there's accelerant in his truck." He blew out a heavy breath. "What if she murdered Roy?"

"That's a stretch," Heather said. "To hear Aidy tell it, Roy made a lot of enemies. Besides, Reagan had no motive for killing him. She'd moved on with her life. Dave seems like a great guy."

"If she convinced Roy to set the fire, he might have threatened to talk afterward. That would be motive enough to silence him."

Heather interlaced her fingers and cracked her knuckles. "Marco, I get the feeling you're talking all around the issue. If there's more to this triangle then you're telling me, I can't help you unless you come clean. Why would Reagan, or Roy for that matter, want to set fire to your restaurant? Was there money involved? Did Reagan invest in your business or something? Or are you still carrying on with her? Whatever it is, I need to know if I'm going to get to the bottom of this before someone else ends up dead."

Marco set his water bottle back down on the bench next to his uneaten sandwich. "She wanted more money. A lot more money. Shares in the restaurant."

Heather scrunched her brows together. "Why were you giving her money in the first place?"

"It wasn't for her." Marco sniffed and stared at the ground in front of him. "It was for our daughter."

25

Heather inhaled a shallow breath as she digested Marco's words. She'd had her suspicions all along that Lucy might be his daughter. This was what Anna had been alluding to when she hinted that Marco and Reagan had a deeper connection than anyone thought. No wonder Roy had been enraged when he discovered the truth.

"How did Roy find out?" Heather asked.

"He grew suspicious that Lucy wasn't his—she doesn't look anything like him. He took a paternity test. When he found out the truth, he went ballistic. That's why he and Reagan split up. He threatened to take her to court and sue her for custody just to expose the truth. He wanted money to keep his mouth shut. I paid up so Anna wouldn't find out."

"I've been giving Reagan money every month for Lucy," Marco went on. "She came to me a few weeks ago and said Roy was blackmailing her again. She needed more money to shut him up. I told her I didn't believe her. You can imagine how well that went over."

Heather rubbed her brow, sifting through the information. Was it possible Reagan had persuaded Roy to set fire to the restaurant when Marco refused to give her more money? Heather chewed on her lip as she pondered the idea. It didn't sit right with her—it verged on fantastical. She threw Marco a sharp look. He hadn't been entirely honest with her either up until now. Could he have schemed with Reagan to set fire to his own restaurant and make it look like an arson attempt in a crazy bid to frame Roy? Marco had quite the temper when he was wound up, and he wouldn't take kindly to being blackmailed, directly or indirectly. Her thoughts scrambled for purchase as she tried to make sense of things. Crime was always about love, money, or revenge—in this case, there seemed to be no clear winner when it came to landing on a motive. And was any of this connected to Lindsay's death?

"Have you shared your suspicions with the police?" Heather asked.

Marco threw her a horrified look. "Reagan's the mother of my child. I don't want to destroy my daughter's life without being sure of my facts. I could be way off base. Roy was a lowlife. Anyone in the circles he hung out in could have bumped him off."

"So why are you telling me this?"

"Because I want you to find out if Reagan was involved in any way in the arson or Roy's death—just be discreet about it." He ran a hand through his hair, a strained expression on his face. "Obviously, I don't want Anna finding out about the affair, but I have to protect my daughter too. If Reagan's capable of murder, I can't have my daughter living with her any longer."

Heather briefly considered telling Marco that Anna already knew about the affair, and possibly even suspected

Lucy was his child. In the end, she decided against it. It was up to Anna to confront him or not.

"You do realize if you'd told me this earlier, Roy might still be alive," she said in a clipped tone, as she got to her feet. "I'll see what I can find out. I'll be in touch."

She could feel Marco's eyes on her as she walked back to her car. She hadn't got the impression that he'd set up the meeting under false pretenses. He seemed genuinely afraid Reagan might be behind the arson. But Heather wasn't in a particularly trusting mood—not after Marco had schemed with Reagan behind her back to pump Violet for information, and hidden the fact that Lucy was his daughter.

She climbed back into her car and texted Aidy. She needed to find out more about Roy Krueger. His girlfriend was as good a place as any to start.

Can you meet me for coffee this afternoon?

If I can bring Trevor. Aidy responded.

Heather sent her a thumbs-up emoji, gritting her teeth as she arranged a time and place. She would have preferred to have Aidy's undivided attention, but she would take what she could get. After that, she would pay a visit to Damien's mother.

A FLUSHED AND frazzled-looking Aidy walked into Darcey's Diner a little after three that afternoon pushing a stroller. "Sorry I'm late," she said, exhaling loudly as she shrugged out of her jacket. "Trevor was being a real pill." She unstrapped him from the stroller and placed him in the highchair at the end of the table, before taking her seat. Heather smiled tentatively at the tear-streaked toddler who immediately pulled his lips into a pout and jerked his face away from her. Aidy scattered some Cheerios on the tray in front of him. Trevor proceeded to chomp his way through them, glaring intermittently at Heather while throwing the occasional glance down at the Cheerios that escaped his clumsy thumb and forefinger pincer grip.

"Thanks for meeting me," Heather said. "How are you doing?"

Aidy shrugged. "If it isn't obvious by now, there wasn't much love lost between me and Roy. I tried to make it work, for Trevor's sake, but Roy was always fooling around. I haven't shed a tear over his death." She cocked her head to one side and looked at Heather quizzically. "Does that make me a monster?"

Heather shook her head. "It makes you human—more honest than most."

Their waitress appeared at their table and took their orders for coffee and pie, even managing to get a smile out of Trevor in the process—which made Heather feel more inadequate than she already did. She pushed the disconcerting thought aside that she was probably going to be a complete failure as an aunt. That was a worry for another day. She had a few months to work on it.

She leaned across the table and looked intently at Aidy. "You know how you said Lucy wasn't Roy's child—do you know whose child she is?"

Aidy's face closed over. "Maybe."

"It's really important for my investigation."

Aidy cast a furtive glance around and then said in a half-whisper. "It's the guy who owns The Sardinian—that fancy Italian restaurant."

"How do you know?" Heather asked, keeping a neutral expression.

A look of apprehension crossed Aidy's face. "I don't want to get in any trouble."

"This is a confidential conversation," Heather assured her. "I have no connection to the police. I'm a private investigator. Believe me, the clients I work for have no interest in you."

Trevor let out a yelp and slapped a fat hand down on the tray table causing the few remaining Cheerios to jitterbug sideways. As if on auto pilot, Aidy tipped some more snacks onto the tray table. "I read the messages on Roy's phone between him and Reagan."

"What did they say?"

Aidy curled her lip. "They were always arguing about money. Roy said stuff like, *she's not my daughter so pay up or I won't shut up.* And she was always going on about how hard it was to get more money out of Marco—that he kept spending it all on jewelry for Anna."

"So Roy was blackmailing Reagan?"

"I guess," Aidy responded, averting her gaze. "A few days before he died, he was complaining because her payment was late."

Their order arrived and Heather gave Aidy a few minutes to enjoy her apple pie before she started up again. "Did Reagan mention anything about the fire at Bella Calabria?"

Aidy's eyes widened. "Do you think she was involved?"

"I don't know. It just seems very convenient that the accelerant was found in Roy's truck after he turned up dead."

Aidy frowned, a spoonful of apple pie halfway to her mouth. "So you think she planted the accelerant in his truck?"

"I think someone did," Heather replied. She swallowed a mouthful of coffee, and tried again to connect with Trevor, who tossed a Cheerio at her before lowering his head and glowering at her from beneath his brows like a bull getting ready to charge.

"Trevor!" Aidy snapped. "Be nice!"

"He's fine," Heather soothed. "Back to the text messages between Roy and Reagan, did anything else strike you as odd?"

Aidy licked her spoon and dropped it on her plate. "To be honest, I didn't pay much attention. I was looking for evidence of Roy cheating on me with someone."

Heather gave her a sympathetic smile. "Did you find anything?"

"You'd better believe it. I found this a few days ago." Aidy fished out her phone. "I air dropped the picture to myself in case he tried to deny it later." She flicked through her photos and then turned the screen so Heather could view it.

Blood drained from her head. The photo was grainy, but the woman with her face angled away from the camera had a thick brown braid of hair hanging over one shoulder.

26

H eather dialed Josh's number as she sat in her car in the parking lot outside Darcey's Diner. To her frustration, her call went straight to voicemail. Josh still hadn't responded to any of the messages she'd sent him. She wanted to bring him up to speed and get his take on things before she confronted Bill Kinney's ex-wife, Judy. It might even be wise to take him along and have him wait in the car. But she couldn't wait any longer to hear back from him. Everything pointed to Damien's mother being the linchpin of the entire case—the woman who'd ordered the flowers and poisoned Sydney. Heather sent Josh a quick text to let him know where she was going and then plugged in the address in her maps app. If Judy Kinney was the mysterious woman at the heart of everything, it was time for Heather to face her.

Armed with the photo Aidy had airdropped to her phone, and with her weapon concealed beneath her jacket, Heather set out on the drive. It was still unclear to her why Judy Kinney's picture was on Roy's phone. Aidy hadn't been able to tell from the grainy photo, but Judy was at least twenty years older than Roy. It didn't seem credible that the two had been romantically attached. A more likely scenario was that she had schemed with him to set fire to Marco's restaurant. Perhaps he had tried to blackmail her afterward, and she'd killed him. Blackmail seemed to be Roy's modus operandi. However it had panned out, he had played a dirty game with two different women and lost.

Twenty minutes later, Heather pulled into the condominium complex on the edge of Davenport where Judy Kinney lived. Nothing about the unremarkable neighborhood suggested she was wealthy enough to be worth blackmailing. On the other hand, she must have got something out of the divorce settlement.

After locking her car, Heather made her way up the steps to the second-floor condo and rang the bell for 2A. When the door opened, she found herself in the uncomfortable position of looking into the eyes of the woman Bill had cheated on with Lindsay. It felt like everything was coming full circle. Connections were firing in all directions, but Heather had yet to put some semblance of order to them. Judy's hair was cut in a sleek blonde bob, but that meant nothing—a wig with a braid could be procured easily enough over the internet nowadays. "Hi, I'm Heather Nelson. Lindsay Robinson was a close friend of mine. I've been helping her mother go through her things and I came across a couple of photos I wanted to ask you about."

The woman's lips remained fastened in a tight line, but a gleam of curiosity lit up her eyes. Heather couldn't tell for sure if Judy recognized her or not. If she did, she was remarkably cool about it.

After a moment of indecision, she stepped aside and invited Heather in. "Just so you know, I never held what happened against your friend. I realize Bill took advantage of her." She led the way into a small but tasteful kitchen-sitting room combo and gestured to a cream-colored tufted chair. "Can I get you something to drink?"

"Some water would be great, thanks," Heather responded, taking the few seconds Judy's back was turned to glance around the space.

Judy handed her a glass of ice water and sat down on a matching chair opposite her. "How did you know Lindsay?"

"We went to school together, all the way from elementary through high school," Heather answered. "We were best friends. We spent most of our free time together, apart from when we were working. As you know, Lindsay worked at your car wash on the weekends. I assume you met her?"

"I don't remember." Judy tilted her head back and eyed Heather appraisingly. "I take it you knew back then about her affair with Bill?"

"I knew of it," Heather conceded. "But I never met him." She paused, eying the water and deciding against risking taking a sip. "I tried to talk Lindsay into ending it. We argued a lot about it, but she insisted they were in love, and that Bill was going to leave you and marry her."

Judy let out a sarcastic laugh. "He left me all right, but I guess he left her too. He moved out of state after I sued for divorce."

Heather nodded, studying her expression. "I know. I tried to contact him."

A flicker of uncertainty crossed Judy's face. "Tried?"

"I found out he passed away recently," Heather said.

Judy gave a stiff nod. "He had pancreatic cancer. I wouldn't wish it on anyone, not even him."

"Did you get to see him again before he died?" Heather asked, feigning a sympathetic air. She had to find out if Bill had told Judy what she had done, or if she had come here on a wild goose chase.

"I had no wish to," Judy said sharply.

"For what it's worth, I'm sorry for the pain you've suffered," Heather said, hoping to steer the conversation around to Damien. Sooner or later, Judy might slip up and say something incriminating.

"It's funny how things ended up," Judy said looking distractedly out the window. "Funny's not really the right word. What I mean is that it's odd they both ended up dying before their time—and within a few months of each other." She turned back to Heather and pinned a steely gaze on her. "Makes you wonder, doesn't it? Some would say they got their just desserts in the end."

"I don't think it works that way. We don't always get justice in this life," Heather said, eying her coolly. "I've learned that in my line of work."

Judy reached for her water. "What line of work are you in?"

"I'm a private investigator—based in LA."

Judy arched a brow. "That sounds exciting. And dangerous. Of course living in LA sounds dangerous to me. I'm a small-town girl myself. I could never live in a big city."

"It's not as exciting as you think," Heather answered. "Most of the time I'm huddled up in my car late at night trying to keep warm. I'm hired to tail a lot of cheating spouses in divorce cases."

Judy smiled coldly. "How ironic. I could have used you back in the day." She crossed her legs and set her glass down on the end table. "So, what are these photos you wanted to ask me about?"

Heather retrieved the photo of Bill and Lindsay from her backpack, and then pulled up the newspaper article of

Damien and his parents on her phone. She held them both out to Judy.

She took the photo of Bill and Lindsay from Heather's hand and studied it wordlessly before glancing at the picture on Heather's phone. "I've always loved this one of Damien. He got player of the year his senior year. Bill and I were so proud of him."

"I wanted to ask you whether Damien knew Lindsay," Heather said. "He was only a year older than her. I wondered if their paths ever crossed."

Judy handed the photos back to Heather. "I suppose he might have seen her at the car wash, but they didn't hang out together." She hesitated, a perturbed frown on her brow. "I still don't understand why you're here."

Heather thought for a moment. Judy Kinney was not a particularly warm person, but Heather was finding it hard to believe she was capable of murder, or even arson. "The truth is, Lindsay's friends hired me to look into her death. We've been receiving threatening messages over the last few months, and one of her friends was poisoned and ended up in hospital. I've been trying to track down all Lindsay's acquaintances to see if they know anything that could be helpful—in particular, if she was being threatened in the weeks before she died." She paused and then added, "Was she in touch with your ex-husband before he passed away?"

A flash of irritation crossed Judy's face. "I wouldn't know. Have you notified the police?"

"They're investigating the poisoning incident, but unfortunately, there's not a lot they can do about the threats."

Judy wrinkled her forehead. "I really don't see how I can help you either."

"It was a long shot, admittedly," Heather said. "I thought Bill might have said something to you before he passed. I need to rule out the possibility that Lindsay was murdered. I don't want to alarm her mother unnecessarily—she's somewhat frail, and Lindsay was her only child. It was hard watching her go through all her old photos."

Judy's expression softened. "That must be very difficult for her, reliving all the memories. Thankfully, I didn't have to take care of Bill's affairs when he passed. Teresa handled it all."

"Teresa?"

Judy pursed her lips in a disapproving manner. "My estranged daughter—Damien's twin."

Heather blinked across at her trying to keep her composure. *Twin?* Somewhere in the recesses of her mind she vaguely recalled Lindsay mentioning once that Bill had college-aged twins. It had never come up again, and, as the relationship had fizzled out a short time later, it had completely slipped Heather's mind. Her chilled skin began to prickle.

"Does ... your daughter live in Davenport too?" Heather asked, trying to inject a calmness she didn't feel into her voice.

"She lives near Buffalo Hills. It's only thirty miles from here, but I haven't seen her in years. She's ... a strange one, but very bright. She was always a big animal lover but, to tell you the truth, she's a bit of a hoarder. Her house is piled high with stuff and it smells like a kennel. I can't bring myself to go over there."

"Perhaps Bill's death will be a first step in you two getting back together," Heather suggested, desperate to keep Judy talking. The more she could find out about Teresa, the better.

Judy let out a snort. "Not likely. She never forgave me for divorcing her father. It was a contentious split. Teresa was in veterinary school at the time and she had to drop out—the divorce ate all our money." She twisted her lips. "Maybe if Bill had been more focused on the business than on his extracurricular activities, we'd have been in a better position."

"So Teresa took her father's side?" Heather prompted.

"At first she did. But after he abandoned us, Damien became very rebellious. He started drinking and hanging out with the wrong crowd. And then ... came the accident. Teresa blamed her father for Damien's death—well, her father and his lover."

27

"Of course, I never told Damien and Teresa who their father cheated on me with," Judy rambled on. "Your friend was only a teenager, after all, and I knew Bill would dump her as soon as the novelty wore off." She broke off and peered at Heather with a perturbed expression on her face. "Are you all right?"

Heather swallowed the rapidly thickening knot in her throat. "I'm fine, thanks. It's just such a ... sad story."

Judy sighed, tucking a strand of blonde hair behind her ear. "It really is. With Bill's passing, I've lost my entire family —more or less. But you've had your own share of grief to deal with. You lost your best friend." She got to her feet and started fussing with the fresh cut flowers in the vase on the end table next to her chair.

Heather rose, taking it as her cue to leave. "I should get going. I appreciate your time."

"Take care of yourself back in LA," Judy said, showing her to the door. "It's a very different world to Iowa."

"Different, but in some ways just the same," Heather replied.

.   .   .

BACK IN HER CAR, she immediately dialed Josh's number. Once again, the phone went straight to voicemail. She thumped her fist on the dashboard in frustration. Why hadn't he called her back? With or without him, she was going to drive out to Buffalo Hills right now and confront Teresa. There was no doubt in her mind that Damien's twin sister was the mysterious stranger with the braided hair. She dug around in her backpack for her laptop and connected it to her phone's hotspot. It didn't take long before she had tracked down Teresa's address in one of her industry databases. After punching the details into her GPS, she put the car in gear.

As she was pulling out of the condominium complex, her phone beeped with an incoming text. She glanced impatiently at the screen. *Josh—finally!* She reached for her phone and opened up the text, staring in confusion as a picture flashed onto her screen—a man tied to a chair, his head flopped forward on his chest.

Her breath came in short, shallow bursts, her thoughts swirling in confused gusts like particles in a dust storm. Breathless with terror, she enlarged the picture. There was no question that it was Josh. He was in a room somewhere, but the picture was too dark to make out any details in the background. Goosebumps pricked her arms, spreading over her skin like fire ants. She couldn't tell if he was dead or alive. If anything happened to him, she would never forgive herself for dragging him into this. A moment later, a second text came through.

If you want to see him again, come alone.

Heather typed frantically back. *Who is this?*

Didn't my mother tell you? I'm the evil twin.

Heather squeezed her eyes shut. *Teresa*! She must have seen her together with Josh and decided to use him as bait. And she had his phone, so she knew all about Heather's visit to Judy. It all made sense now. It was as Heather had feared all along—Lindsay's so-called accident had been no accident. It had been a meticulously planned murder. And Teresa wasn't finished yet.

A chill rippled across Heather's shoulders as the stark truth hit her. *Heather has killed before. She'll do it again.* There was no doubt in her mind that Teresa knew everything. And now she had Josh tied up and helpless, completely at her mercy. One-by-one, she was coming after Heather's friends. Maybe she assumed they all knew she had left Damien to die and had covered it up all these years. Instinctively, Heather's hand went to the concealed weapon beneath her shirt. She couldn't afford to take any chances. Teresa was clearly unstable. She had demonstrated as much, and her mother had confirmed it. She had also proved she was dangerous. It might already be too late to save Josh.

Mustering her resolve, Heather floored the gas pedal, and headed toward the town of Buffalo Hills. As she drove, she tried to collect her thoughts. She needed to stay calm and treat this as a run-of-the-mill assignment, distance herself from the emotional side of what was happening. If she thought of Josh as her friend, instead of simply another client, she would lose the cool edge that had served her well in her investigations over the years. Allowing the emotions she was feeling inside free rein would make her vulnerable. She had no choice but to tackle the situation like every other job she was hired to do. Josh's life depended on it.

Taking a few deep breaths, she tried to mentally prepare herself for the inevitable showdown that awaited her. Ultimately, Damien's sister would require her pound of flesh.

But Heather had a hunch she wouldn't be in a rush to finish what she'd started. First, she would want to talk her way through it, explaining with relish exactly how she had figured out who Lindsay was, how she'd pulled off her *accidental death*, and how she was going about picking off her friends one-by-one. No doubt, she would try to justify everything she was doing. As deranged as she was, Teresa probably believed she was acting rationally by avenging her brother's death. Heather could understand only too well the pain that fueled her anger, and the things it could drive a person to do.

Blowing through a red light, she struggled to get her head straight. She would play Teresa's game in the hopes of lowering her defenses—compliment her genius, feed her ego, all the while waiting for the right moment to overpower her. She wouldn't use her gun unless that was what it took to free Josh. Maybe she could persuade Teresa to let Josh go and let her take his place—although he didn't look like he was in any state to drive away. Teresa must have drugged him or something. How else could she have overpowered him? And how on earth had she lured him there in the first place?

As Heather left the suburbs behind and ventured farther into farmland, her thoughts drifted back to that fateful night twenty years earlier when she had pursued Damien to his death. This time fate had turned the tables on her. Her life would soon be in the hands of his twin—a woman whose desire for revenge had festered for two decades until, at last, she had found a target on which to unleash her hatred. Heather had no idea what to expect at Teresa's place— whether she would be walking into a trap, or whether Josh was even alive. Regardless, she owed it to him to get there as quickly as she could. She would do whatever it took to save him. He didn't deserve to die for what she'd done.

It had finally caught up with her in the worst possible way. Deep down she had always known this day would come—she just hadn't known what form it would take. Now, she was about to find out.

28

Teresa opened the door of her father's apartment to see two removal techs from the Gillpatrick Mortuary standing on the steps. Their expressions were a smooth blend of sympathetic and grave. "I'm Tyler Coffman," one of the men said. "We spoke on the phone. Once again, I'm very sorry for your loss. This is my associate, Nick DuBois. We're here to pick up your father's remains."

Wordlessly, Teresa led them to the bedroom where her father had expired after she had rejected the hospice nurse's recommendation to transfer him to a hospital. The last thing she had wanted was a hospital stay with needless interventions dragging out his death any longer than necessary. She had to get back to her animals.

"Does your father have any valuables on him?" Tyler asked.

Teresa let out a snort of laughter. "Have you seen this dump? Does it look to you like he's leaving any valuables behind?" She ignored the reproachful tilt of Tyler's brow. Playing the part of a grieving daughter was proving more irritating than she'd anticipated. Her father certainly hadn't grieved the loss of her veterinary career, or the breakup of their family, or even Damien's death. They'd had to pick up the pieces after he'd left them—broke, in every sense of the word.

Damien had struggled the most. He had both hated his father for what he'd done and yearned for him at the same time. He had always been headstrong, but he started drinking heavily after their father walked away. Everything fell apart after that. Not even Damien's death had brought her father back into her life. He had attended his son's funeral and left abruptly after the burial. She hadn't seen her father again until two days ago when she'd driven out to Wisconsin after the hospice nurse called to let her know he was on death's door. She would have preferred it if he'd passed before she got here, but he'd stubbornly lingered on, seemingly determined to try and forge some last-minute sham of a relationship with her. She hadn't reciprocated.

"My associate and I will do a quick check to make sure your father's not wearing any jewelry, or rings. Sometimes things get overlooked," Tyler explained, in an infuriatingly gentle tone. "Would you like a few moments with your father?"

Teresa twisted her lips. She'd had all the time with him she could stomach. "No, that won't be necessary."

Tyler gestured discreetly to Nick who moved the gurney they had brought with them into position next to the bed.

"If you'd prefer, you can wait outside for this part of the process," Tyler said, pulling on a pair of rubber gloves.

Teresa gave a curt nod and left them to it. Not because it troubled her to see her father wrapped in plastic and loaded onto the gurney like a piece of meat, but because her face was aching from faking a grieved expression. Minutes later, she watched as his body was wheeled out of the house to the van waiting to take his remains to the funeral home for cremation. She felt nothing inside. Just like she'd felt nothing when her father's lawyer had notified her that she was the sole beneficiary to his estate—what little there was left of it.

She would never forgive her parents for destroying her life. Their divorce had sent her world spiraling into an abyss of hardship and bitter disappointment. They had never shared the gory details of her father's affair with her or Damien, only that he had cheated. Afterward, they had learned he had mismanaged the car wash business so badly that it owed more than it was worth. Her mother had been convinced he was trying to hide money from her. She'd hired lawyer after lawyer in an attempt to squeeze him dry. But it was only herself she pushed to the brink of financial ruin. The embarrassment and shame Teresa felt at having to drop out of veterinary school had scarred her deeply. It was the only thing she had ever truly wanted—a career working with the animals she loved.

"Will you be attending the cremation?" Tyler asked, blinking solemnly at her.

"No," Teresa replied. "That would be too ..." Inconvenient came to mind, among several other words, but she restrained herself. " ... too troubling for me."

Tyler inclined his head. "I'll let the mortuary director know your wishes. My condolences once again."

Teresa closed the door behind him and let out a sigh of relief as she watched the mortuary van drive off down the road.

She turned and cast a disparaging look around the space. The one-bedroom apartment her father had been living in was a hovel compared to the home she had grown up in. She was almost certain she would find nothing of value here. Initially, she'd been hoping to score something she could sell, but the contents would likely prove to be worth less than the cost of cleaning the place up. At least she could get the deposit back. The apartment manager had indicated that she would also have to clean out the storage area where her father kept moldy boxes of old files from the business. Another chore she didn't relish undertaking. She made her way to the kitchen and poured herself a shot of vodka. No time like the present. She might as well begin sorting through things and tossing whatever she could. The sooner she got back to Iowa and her beloved pets, the better. She hadn't planned on being gone for three straight days. Her neighbor's kids were coming over twice a day to feed the dogs, but they wouldn't give them the attention they deserved. No one loved them like she did.

Grabbing a handful of trash bags, she walked back to her father's bedroom. She yanked open the drawer in the nightstand and poked through the contents with disgust. Reading glasses, motorcycle magazines, used tissues, miscellaneous receipts, a handful of coins, and a bottle of melatonin. It only affirmed what she'd already suspected— the apartment contained nothing more than the worthless remnants of a life that no one would mourn. She quickly swept the contents into a trash bag and then closed the drawer back up. A plastic storage tub beneath the bed revealed an electric blanket which appeared to be missing the power cord, and an extra pillow, yellowed with age. She added both items to the trash bag. Next, she opened the closet and rummaged through the clothes. Most of them were in decent shape, if somewhat out of style. Someone in the apartment complex might be able to use them. She would leave them on the doorstep and tape a *free* sign to the door. It would save her the trouble of hauling them out of here. When she was done loading the clothes into a bag, she started on the shoes. The tiny closet didn't take long to empty. She stood and stretched, eying the shelf above. Judging by the dust that had accumulated, it hadn't been touched in a while. She stood on her tiptoes and lifted down a shoebox, wrinkling up her nose and sneezing as dust billowed down on her face.

She sank down on the bed and removed the lid. The box held a jumble of miscellaneous items; everything from newspaper articles about the car wash business over the years, to a certified copy of her parents' divorce decree. Teresa lifted it out and stared at it with revulsion. That single sheet of paper represented everything that had been stolen from her. In a sudden fit of rage she began shredding it, grinding her teeth in the process. When she was done, she scowled down at the pieces scattered over the floor like the broken shards of her life. Her hatred hadn't died with her father, it had only intensified. Vaulting to her feet, she strode into the kitchen and poured herself another shot. She needed something to calm her rage. Just until she could get through the cleanup and blaze a trail out of here. She should have made her mother handle her father's affairs as penance for everything she'd put them through—frittering away every last dime they had on lawyers. The estate wasn't worth collecting on. She was already regretting wasting her time driving out here.

After a few minutes, she returned to the bedroom and picked up where she had left off. Gingerly, she lifted down another shoebox. Just like the first one, it contained a hodgepodge of items collected over the years, none of which were of any significance to her. Halfway through tossing the contents, she pulled out a folded piece of blue construction paper. Written on the back were the words: *Damien, kinder-garten*. Teresa smoothed the paper out on her lap and stared at the four crayon stick figures with elongated fingers and oversized smiles, along with the obligatory sun in the background shining down on them. She let out a snort of disgust. An idyllic lineup that bore no resemblance to how things had turned out for the Kinney clan. Teresa flattened her lips, a familiar rage seething inside. She crumpled the paper in her fist and tossed it into the trash bag. She was sick and tired of going through her father's belongings. If he had thought any of it would mean something to her, it didn't.

She reached for the rest of the papers in the box and flung them into the trash bag without even glancing at them. Something fell out and rolled away from her. She got down on her hands and knees and peered under the bed, her eyes widening when she spotted the gold band. She picked it up and twisted it around in her fingers as she read the inscription: *Judy, 06/07/75*. Her father had actually kept his wedding ring—more likely, forgotten it was in there. Teresa pocketed it. Gold at least had trade-in value, unlike memories.

She tossed the empty shoebox in the trash bag and retrieved the remaining box from the shelf. Perched on the edge of the bed, she rummaged aimlessly through the contents. It was mostly old photographs, and she had no interest in reliving the lies of her childhood. She flipped through several pictures and then came to a sudden halt at one photo in particular. She lifted it out and studied it. Her heart slugged against her ribs.

It was her father—standing in front of his car wash business, his arm snaked around the waist of one of his young blonde employees who was leaning up to kiss him.

29

Teresa propped the photo up against a stack of books on the kitchen table and slumped down in a chair without taking her eyes off it. In her right hand, she held an empty shot glass. She'd lost count of how many drinks she'd put away, but it didn't matter. She was celebrating—a double celebration. A toast to her father's death, but also to the gift he'd inadvertently left her. *Revenge*. Against all odds, he had left her something of value after all. The blonde in the photo was the reason Teresa's life had ended up the way it had. She should have been Teresa Kinney, *Doctor of Veterinary Medicine*. Instead, she'd been reduced to working as a game warden—or *conservation officer*, as the Department of Natural Resources liked to dress it up as. Blondie was also the reason her father's meager estate amounted to a dozen or so black trash bags and an obsolete wedding ring. More important, Blondie was the reason Damien was dead. She had taken his father away from him at a time when he needed him most. He had fallen apart as a result. Whether she knew it or not, she was responsible for Damien's death.

Teresa exhaled slowly in and out, trying to restrain herself from poking the girl's eyes out with a ballpoint pen. She couldn't allow herself to vent her rage—she needed to preserve the photo. At least until she had identified who the girl was, which shouldn't be too hard. She was wearing an Elite Finish uniform which indicated that she'd been an employee at one point.

All Teresa had to do was go through her father's business files until she found his old employee records. She wouldn't need anything more than a last name and a social security number to track the girl down. But it would have to wait until morning. It was too dark down in that musty old storage unit to begin the process of digging through the boxes tonight. Besides, she was too drunk. Shakily, she poured herself another shot. It had been a stroke of good luck that she hadn't tossed out that final shoebox. It was meant to be. Things worked out for a reason. Blondie would get what was coming to her—sadly, two decades too late to save Damien. All Teresa could do now was take what she'd been given and avenge her brother's death.

IT WAS close to ten o'clock the next morning before she woke up. She uncurled her cramped legs from the couch where she had spent an uncomfortable night, groaning as she sat up and assessed her condition. She had a throbbing headache from overindulging in vodka, and a kink in her neck from lying wrong on the lumpy cushions. As uncomfortable as the couch was, she hadn't been able to bring herself to sleep in the same bed that her father had died in.

She padded across the floor and switched on the coffeemaker, her eyes going straight to the photo she had left propped up on the table. During the course of the night it had tipped over and was lying face down—a symbolic nod to the destruction Teresa was about to unleash. Whatever charmed existence Blondie was currently leading was about to come to a screeching halt. And Teresa knew exactly how that would play out. But first, she had to find out who the woman was and track her down.

After downing a mug of cheap coffee, she grabbed the keys to her father's apartment and made her way down to his storage locker in the communal basement. After fiddling with the key for several frustrating minutes, she managed to work the padlock open. She wrinkled her nose in disgust at the fusty scent that tickled her nostrils—not unlike the stench of death itself—from the archived life now boxed up in front of her. She was beginning to regret not having brought some gloves with her.

With an air of resolve, she opened the first mold-speckled cardboard file box and got to work. An hour later, she had barely made a dent in the stack that reached to the ceiling. Claustrophobia was closing in. She had no idea how people could spend all day every day at meaningless jobs going through paperwork, filing it, researching it, and ultimately adding to the never-ending mountains of it that filled the planet. She let out a disgusted sigh. She was sick of being trapped in the gloomy basement. She desperately missed her animals—her own little family. With them, she could close the door on the outside world and bask in their unconditional love. Not the kind of broken human love that was dispensed or withdrawn at will and could disappear one day without any warning.

The sound of shuffling caught her attention, and she threw a sharp glance over her shoulder. An elderly man with a cane was making his way toward her. She groaned inwardly. Her patience was wearing thin and the last thing she needed was an aging cripple wasting her time.

"You must be Bill's daughter," the man said, raising a gnarled hand in greeting. "I'm sorry for your loss."

Teresa cocked her head to one side. "You know, I've never really understood why they call family members beneficiaries at a time of such ... *loss*," she said, with an edge of thinly veiled sarcasm. She gestured to the boxes around her. "Some benefit, right? I get to clean up his mess."

Confusion pooled in the old man's rheumy eyes. He blinked uncertainly back at her, as if reassessing the situation. "Well, I shall certainly miss my chats with your father. He loved to talk about his kids, you know."

"I suppose that's all you can do when you don't have a relationship with them."

The old man cleared his throat. "I can see you're busy. I'll leave you to it." He raised his cane in parting and hobbled back down the corridor and out of sight.

Teresa straightened up and massaged her neck. Sitting hunched over these boxes was not helping whatever she'd done to it last night. She needed to speed this process up and get out of here. Maybe she should try a different strategy. She got to her feet and balanced on a file box, then began tossing boxes to the floor, not caring if they landed upside down or whether the contents spilled. Stepping back down to the floor, she opened the first box at her feet. The task was taking longer than she had expected because nothing was organized.

After sifting through multiple boxes of everything from vendor contracts to utility bills, she tackled another batch of boxes and stumbled, at last, on what she was looking for—a box of employee records. She held her breath as she lifted out the first folder. *Anderson, Tonya*. Flicking through the files, she determined that she'd found the records for *A* through *H*. With no idea what Blondie's name was, Teresa had no choice but to start at the beginning and work her way through the files to the end.

By the time she made it through the second box containing *I* through *P*, her frustration had reached boiling point. Her head was pounding like a bad rock concert. She needed more coffee. Better yet, another shot of vodka might be in order. If it wasn't for the fact that she had a three-and-a-half-hour drive back home ahead of her, she would be sorely tempted.

Gritting her teeth, she resolved to buckle down and finish what she had started. After discarding several more boxes of receipts and advertising brochures, she finally discovered the remaining employee files, *R* through *Z*. One-by-one, she pulled them out and flicked through them searching for a faded head shot that would match the girl in the photo. Several of the passport-sized photos had worked their way free of the paperclip attaching them to the employment application and were lying loose in the file, which only dragged the process out even further.

As her discard pile grew larger—Raines, Ramirez, Rassi, Rebholz, Reed, Reuter, Ritter, Rivera, Robertson—her frustration mounted. She glanced at the name on the next file in her hand—Robinson, Lindsay. She flicked it open, poised to add it to the discard pile. Her breath caught in her throat.

Blondie smiled back at her from the pages of her résumé like the cat who'd got the cream.

30

Armed with all the information she needed, Teresa left her father's storage locker in disarray and hurried back upstairs to the apartment to pack up her stuff. She no longer cared about getting the measly deposit back from the landlord. The inherited mess was his problem now. She had everything she wanted in hand. As soon as she got back home, she would throw all her efforts into hunting down Lindsay Robinson and punishing her for destroying her life, her dreams, and her family. She would begin by looking up the old address in Lindsay's employee file. There was a chance her parents still lived there, and she could get the information on Lindsay's current whereabouts from them directly. If not, it wouldn't be too hard to find out where Lindsay had moved to now that Teresa had all of her personal information at her disposal. And once she found her, she would hatch a plan for revenge.

The trip back to her home outside of Buffalo Hills seemed interminably long, and the requisite stop for groceries in Davenport added another forty minutes to the drive, but at last she turned off the main road and onto the long dirt lane up to the modest farmhouse she had bought a decade or so ago with the money she had managed to save from her game warden gig.

She pulled her car into the barn, sending several feral cats scurrying to hide. After gathering up her overnight bag and groceries from the back seat, she made her way into the house. The dogs in the back yard erupted, pawing at the door to get in.

"All right, all right, calm down guys," Teresa said, setting the bags of groceries down on the kitchen table. She opened the back door, and her six dogs came tearing into the kitchen in full force, yapping and barking over one another in their excitement at seeing her. She knelt down, rubbing each of their ears in turn, letting them lick their approval all over her face. "I missed you too." When the dogs had satisfied themselves that she was back to stay, she refilled their water bowls and gave them each a rib bone from the freezer to chew on.

After putting away the groceries, she sent her neighbor a quick text to let her know she'd returned and that she'd drop off some cash for the kids in the morning. She didn't want them coming round to pester her for their money. Not that she intended to pay them much when all they'd had to do was get the dog food from the barn and fill the bowls in the pen twice a day.

Sinking down on the couch with a can of Coke, she took a long sip before pulling Lindsay Robinson's file out of her duffel bag. She eyed it with pleasure, a tingling feeling surfing through her veins like a powerful drug. The file wasn't very thick, which was hardly surprising. Lindsay had only been a part-time employee at the car wash her senior year of high school. Teresa skimmed through her personal details again, committing everything to memory. If she was to move in Lindsay's circles to get close to her, she needed to know everything about her.

When she was done perusing the file, she drained the last of her Coke, and got to her feet. It was time to check on her other babies—they would be stirring by now. She walked over to the door at the top of the basement stairs and unlocked it before turning back around to address her dogs. "Stay!" she commanded them. Apart from a soft whimper, there was no resistance to her command from the pack. She had been strict about their training in this area. They were never allowed to follow her down to the basement, under any circumstances. She simply couldn't take the risk—one or other of her beloved pets was bound to end up dead. She loved all her animals, but she understood only too well that the hostile dispositions of her solitary basement menagerie were not compatible with her canine companions.

After switching on the light, she closed the door behind her and descended the wooden steps. It was dark down in the basement, with only one narrow rectangular window at ground level at the far end. The inhabitants preferred it that way. They also liked it warm, which is why she kept the temperature at a constant seventy-six degrees. It was the only room Teresa had remodeled when she moved into the farmhouse—going so far as to install a new boiler and a separate heating zone to accommodate its residents. She had also taken the time to watch a YouTube video on how to frost a windowpane to make sure her neighbors' kids couldn't see into the basement. Kids were notoriously nosy, and they talked too much—a dangerous combination in this case.

"I'm back, Empress," Teresa crooned to the pit viper curled up in the glass enclosure closest to the stairs. "Are you hungry?" She was relieved to see that the heat lamps were all functioning normally. She typically checked everything on a daily basis, even though her basement babies only ate once a week. It had been years since she'd spent a night away from them. But, as it turned out, it had been worth the trip.

She walked over to the freezer in the corner of the room and retrieved several packets of rodents which she placed in a basin of warm water in the sink. While she waited for them to defrost, she crossed over to the enclosure that contained her prized krait snake. It had been the hardest one of her collection to procure, but she didn't regret the extra effort it had taken. No matter how long she spent staring at him, his striking black and yellow bands never ceased to take her breath away. "How's my handsome boy, Achilles, today?"

Achilles ignored her. As with all her other nocturnal pets, he preferred to sleep away the daylight hours, undisturbed by mortals. After admiring him for several minutes, she moved on to the third floor-length enclosure which housed her black mamba, Medusa—her most recent addition, and by far her most aggressive. Teresa handled her with extreme caution, relying on her snake hook and heavy-duty reptile grabber to move her whenever she needed to clean the enclosure. Medusa was fascinating to watch, opening her inky-black mouth to hiss at Teresa when she stared at her for too long. Of all the snakes she had owned, Medusa was by far the most active and fast-moving, her lithe gunmetal gray body rearing up to strike in the blink of an eye.

The final enclosure contained her timber rattlesnakes, Brom and Beretta. Teresa had a special bond with them. She was immensely proud of the fact that, unlike her non-native snakes, she hadn't purchased them over the internet but had captured them in the wild. It was strictly against policy for a game warden to trap a reptile or animal and bring it home, but the long hours she spent alone on the job ensured there was no one looking over her shoulder to enforce the policy.

A smile tugged at her lips as she watched her rattlers sleep curled up on top of one another. She was fairly certain, based on the disparate size of their tails, that she'd managed to snag a male and a female and she was hoping they might breed. "Grub's up, my lovelies," Teresa mouthed to them through the glass. Grabbing her tongs, she fetched a rat from the plastic bowl in the sink, and dangled it over Brom, letting his head touch the bait. In a lightning strike, he snatched the meal from the outstretched tongs and slithered into the corner of the enclosure with it. "Patience, Beretta, my love," Teresa soothed. "You're next."

After feeding each of her snakes in turn, Teresa double checked the heat lamps and then wound her way back up the stairs to the kitchen, taking care to lock the door to the basement after her. She left the key in the lock as she usually did when she was home by herself. Hungry after her long trip, she fixed herself a sandwich and sat down in front of the television to eat. She flipped through several channels, but she couldn't focus. She was too busy anticipating Lindsay's demise. A plan was formulating that thrilled her to the core.

31

The following morning, Teresa drove to her neighbor's house two miles down the road. She rang the doorbell and when no one answered, she jammed an envelope with some cash in the doorframe. With that taken care of, she climbed back in her car and typed Lindsay Robinson's old address into her maps app. She was studiously ignoring the numerous irate messages on her phone from her father's landlord. She had to remain focused on her mission, and that didn't allow for distractions in the form of an angry chump wanting to vent his frustrations about the mess she had left him. He could keep his deposit and haul out the trash himself.

Forty-five minutes later, Teresa pulled up outside a tired-looking house in a quiet suburb. She sat in the car for a moment watching the building for any sign of movement. There was no vehicle in the driveway, but it didn't mean to say no one was home. She glanced at her face in the mirror one last time and then smoothed down her shirt before climbing out of the car. She had taken care with her appearance that morning and applied some makeup for the first time in as far back as she could remember. Granted, she had found it buried in a bathroom drawer, and it had already expired and would likely give her a horrible rash, but it was important to look presentable if she was to pass herself off as an old friend of Lindsay's.

She walked up to the front door and rang the doorbell, tapping her foot impatiently as she waited—ill-at-ease in the unfamiliar heels that were a far cry from the kangaroo boots she usually donned on a daily basis. She was about to ring the doorbell again when a frail voice called out, "Just a minute!"

At last, the door creaked open and an elderly woman on a walker peered out at her.

Teresa's lips curved into a smile. "Hi, I'm looking for Lindsay Robinson. I'm a cycling friend of hers from way back. I live in Boston now but I'm here for a visit and I wanted to look her up."

The woman's face brightened. "Lindsay doesn't actually live here anymore. I'm her mother, Pam." Her papery brow wrinkled. "What did you say your name was?"

"Mary," Teresa blurted out. It was a common enough name. Hopefully, common enough that it wouldn't arouse the woman's curiosity. "We didn't attend the same high school, but we competed in the same cycling league." She fished Lindsay's employee file headshot out of her purse and passed it to Pam. "This is the last photo I have of her."

"Oh my!" Pam chuckled. "That is an old one. She looks so young there. Lindsay normally works until five, but I can give you her address, if you want."

"That would be wonderful. I'm so looking forward to connecting with her again."

"Let me jot it down for you," Pam said, reaching for a pad and pen on the hall table just inside the front door.

Teresa tried to curb her irritation as the woman painstakingly wrote out the address with a shaking hand before passing it to her. She scanned the spidery script to make sure it was legible and then stretched her lips into another phony smile. "Wonderful. Thank you, Pam. I can't wait to see Lindsay's face when I turn up on her doorstep."

"Well, I'm sure you two cyclists will have plenty to catch up on." Pam hesitated and then added, "You have such beautiful hair, dear."

Teresa flicked her heavy braid over her shoulder. "I've had it this way since high school. Probably time for a change."

As she hurried back to her car, she could hardly tamp down her excitement. It had all been so incredibly easy. Handed to her on the proverbial platter. She would take it as a sign that it was meant to be.

32

Over the course of the next few months, Teresa spent every spare minute familiarizing herself with the intimate details of Lindsay Robinson's life: her daily schedule, her training regimen, how she spent her weekends, her favorite attire, which friends she socialized with, the places she liked to hang out. They had more in common than Teresa had realized. Lindsay was also a huge fan of the outdoors and wide-open spaces—in fact, she seemed to spend the bulk of her free time cycling, often taking off on forty- or fifty-mile bike rides.

Clearly, she was also an animal lover. Each morning at 6:00 a.m. on the dot she left her house to walk her miniature Australian Shepherd and Jack Russell terrier. It was the one splinter in her plan that nagged at Teresa. The unfortunate reality was that by the time she was finished with Lindsay, the dogs would likely end up at the local animal shelter. She tried not to think too much about their fate as she went about finalizing her plans.

After gathering her data, she considered the various

options open to her. The fact that Lindsay spent an inordinate amount of time alone in the outdoors made her an easy target for an *unfortunate accident*. There were a variety of catastrophes that could befall a person who hiked and biked in solitude. In the end, Teresa elected to go with a cycling accident—the obvious choice and therefore the least likely to raise any red flags in the aftermath. Of course, it wouldn't end there—she had decided on a particularly fitting finale for Lindsay.

When the day finally arrived, Teresa was more than ready. After feeding her dogs their evening meal, she calmly set about gathering up the supplies she would need. On Sunday evenings, Lindsay typically biked along the Great River trail at dusk, well after most folks had disbanded and headed home for the night. She was disciplined in her training regimen—a creature of habit, which would prove to be her downfall. Teresa had already walked the route several times and picked out the best possible spot for the accident to occur. It was an area that provided plenty of cover for her to hide but was also close to an entrance which made for an easy getaway afterward. More important, this particular section of the trail had just enough of an incline to ensure that Lindsay wouldn't go flying past her before she had a chance to enact her plan.

The last thing Teresa did before leaving the house was bag up Brom and Beretta. It was hard knowing that she wouldn't see them again after tonight, but she couldn't deny that after playing their part they would have earned their freedom. After loading up her car, she drove slowly down the lane to the main road, centering herself by focusing her thoughts on Damien. He was the reason she had gone to all this trouble.

A sense of calm about the task that lay ahead enveloped Teresa as she pulled out onto the main road. She would take the time to explain to Lindsay in detail the extent of the destruction she had wrought on the Kinney family. Lindsay Robinson would die understanding something of the pain and chaos she had caused in the lives she had taken little thought of when she'd brazenly seduced their father. Perhaps she would be remorseful—not that it would spare her the sentence Teresa had already passed. Lindsay Robinson was too far gone for an eleventh-hour pardon.

When she reached the deserted parking lot by the entrance to the trail, Teresa backed her car into the closest spot to allow for a smooth getaway, and then pulled on her gloves. After donning her backpack, she carefully lifted out the sack containing Brom and Beretta, along with her snake handling tools, and made her way to the designated spot. The fall air was crisp, and she shivered in the breeze that was picking up. A yellow-throated warbler in a nearby tree chirped its disapproval at her late arrival.

"Sorry, little guy," Teresa called up to the bird. "I have important business to take care of tonight. After that, I'll be on my way." She set down her backpack, reptile sack, and tools, and checked to make sure her flashlight was working. It was already dusk, and she was well aware that it could take some time for Lindsay to die. She screwed her snake handling hook onto the end of the detachable extension pole and tested how far away she would need to position herself in order to reach the wheel of the bike with it.

Satisfied with the logistics of her plan, she checked the time again. Fifteen minutes to spare, give or take. Brom and Beretta were waiting in their bag behind her, next to a rock she had selected to inflict just enough damage to stun

Lindsay into submission. Settling into the brush in a sniper position, Teresa stilled her breathing, modeling her reptiles' behavior as she waited in the darkness for her unsuspecting prey.

At the whoosh of tires on the trail, she tightened her grip on the handle of her hook and took several shallow breaths. She had practiced lying in the brush and listening for the sound of Lindsay's bike approaching several times over the past weeks, counting down exactly how far away she was from the incline. Teresa had learned the skill of waiting for the perfect moment to strike by studying Medusa. *Don't be impatient, but don't hesitate once your prey is within reach.* The bike rolled ever closer. Three ... two ... one ...

Lindsay's surprised scream pierced the evening air as she flew over the handle bars, the bike skidding out from beneath her. Before she had a chance to react, Teresa was towering over her, swinging the rock. Lindsay's eyes widened in horror, but her frantic attempt to roll out of reach at the last minute was fruitless. The rock connected with the side of her head—hard enough to incapacitate her without killing her. She let out a gasp, her eyes glazing over as she flopped back down in the dirt, blood pouring from her ear. Teresa wasted no time tossing the rock and grabbing Lindsay by the ankle. She dragged her into the brush and then went back to retrieve her bicycle. If any straggling joggers or cyclists happened by, there would be nothing to see on the trail as the last dregs of daylight dissipated. She quickly dismantled the extension pole and packed it away. To her irritation, the hook had snapped off and gone flying into the brush somewhere.

Teresa retrieved a coil of rope from her backpack, and expertly secured Lindsay's hands and feet. Her eyes fluttered open, and she blinked uncomprehendingly up at the sky, clearly stunned from the blow. She moaned softly, too weak to resist as Teresa stuffed a rag into her mouth. After propping her flashlight up against her backpack, she sat down on a tree stump, eying Lindsay dispassionately. Despite the fact that her enemy was in a vulnerable position, Teresa was under no illusion that she was entirely helpless and incapacitated. Lindsay Robinson was an athlete, fit and strong, and would undoubtedly attempt to fight for her life when she rallied enough for the adrenalin to kick in. Teresa would have to watch her back—she hadn't wanted to tie her up too tightly in case it left any telltale marks.

Lindsay's eyes flicked to Teresa once more, and then to her surroundings, as if assessing the predicament she found herself in and calculating her chances of escape.

"I'm sure you have questions," Teresa drawled. "We've got all the time in the world so no need to rush. Get your wind back first."

Lindsay mumbled something unintelligible, straining to spit out the rag in her mouth.

Teresa let out an amused snort. "You do realize I can't understand a word you're saying? It's not that I don't want to hear you out. After all, you deserve a chance to address the jury. But can I trust you not to scream if I remove the rag from your mouth?"

Lindsay wriggled around, attempting once again to dislodge the rag.

Teresa let out an exaggerated sigh and got to her feet. "I can see you're eager to start talking, but you're not compliant yet, so let's go over the ground rules." She walked over to her backpack and lifted the reptile sack lying next to it containing Brom and Beretta. "Do you know what I have in here?" she asked, holding the bag aloft.

Lindsay shook her head and then winced, as though the very movement sent waves of pain throughout her body.

Teresa smirked. "No, of course you don't. Trust me, there's a good reason you're not going to scream when I remove the rag from your mouth." Cautiously, she loosened the top of the sack and lowered the reptile grabber inside. A distinctive rattling instantly filled the night air, followed by an eerie silence, as if every creature in the vicinity had heard the warning and taken heed.

Lindsay's eyes were frantic with fear. She attempted to dig her heels into the dirt and push herself farther away from Teresa.

"There's really no point in exerting yourself," Teresa said, shaking her head. "You're not going anywhere. Why don't we just have a civil conversation instead?"

Lindsay gave a tentative jerk of her chin.

"Excellent," Teresa said, tightening the mouth of the reptile sack back up and setting it aside before hunkering down and yanking the rag from Lindsay's mouth. She put a finger to her lips in warning. "Remember what happens if you scream." Sitting back down on the stump, she traced the end of the reptile grabber in the dirt in front of her. "Do you know who I am?"

"No," Lindsay croaked out.

Teresa gave a thoughtful nod. "I believe you. In fact, I didn't know who you were either until a few months ago when my estranged father passed away in Wisconsin. I was named the sole beneficiary of his paltry fortune." She gave a hollow laugh. "To tell you the truth, it was hardly worth the gas it took to drive there. Or so I thought, until I stumbled on a nugget among the trash he left me—a photograph of you." She licked her lips, watching the confused expression on Lindsay's face. She still hadn't connected the dots. It really had meant that little to her.

"Who are you?" Lindsay rasped. "Why are you doing this?"

Teresa leaned forward and stuck her face up close to her. "I'm Bill Kinney's daughter and you destroyed my life."

33

Lindsay's eyes bulged. She shrank back from Teresa's face, her body shaking. "I ... I didn't even know who you were back then. Your father took advantage of me. I was only seventeen when I went to work for him—a minor in his employment. I could have pressed charges."

"You might as well have," Teresa snarled. "You destroyed our entire family."

"I'm truly sorry for the pain I caused," Lindsay whimpered. "That was never my intention. I was naive. I ... I believed every word your father told me. He said his marriage was over before he met me—that he loved me. We were going to get married after I graduated."

Teresa cocked her head to one side. "How touching. Funny thing is, he told us he loved us too. Just not enough to stay with us, apparently."

"He left me as well," Lindsay whispered, her lip trembling.

"But he didn't leave you broke, did he? Your little affair that you're so dismissive of unleashed a lifetime of consequences for my family. You broke up my parents' marriage. They had to sell the business to pay off their debts. We lost everything—*I* lost everything. They couldn't afford to pay my tuition anymore. I had to drop out of veterinary school. Do you have any idea how hard I had to work to get accepted to begin with?"

Lindsay suppressed a sob. "I'm sorry for everything that happened to you. I had no idea. He never talked about you. I never heard from your father again."

Teresa narrowed her eyes at her. "Do you even know my name?"

"I ... I don't remember."

"It's Teresa. Do you know my twin brother's name?"

Lindsay shook her head, a tear sliding down her cheeks.

"Damien. Say it! *Say his name!*"

"Damien! I'm sorry, Teresa. I truly am. I'll do whatever you want. I'll apologize to Damien too. Just please, untie me and let me go."

Teresa twisted the front of Lindsay's shirt in her fist and shook her. "That phony apology of yours to save your own skin is twenty years too late. Damien's dead, thanks to you. When my father abandoned us, it crushed him. He went off the rails—drinking and partying. He crashed his truck into a tree and died a few months later."

A gasp escaped Lindsay's lips, the whites of her eyes reflecting terror.

Teresa shook her loose and sat back down on the tree stump. "Which brings me to why you and I are here tonight. My family paid the ultimate price because of you, and now you're going to pay the equivalent in return."

"No!" Lindsay shrieked. "Please—"

"Keep your voice down!" Teresa reached for the reptile

bag and dangled it over her. "Have you forgotten what's in here?"

Lindsay opened and shut her mouth a couple of times before giving an acquiescing nod. "Teresa, listen to me, please. We both got a raw deal. We were kids back then. What happened was your father's fault. Surely you can see that."

"Believe me, I'm under no illusions about him. But you were the other half of the problem."

"I'm sorry. I don't know what more I can say to—"

"There's nothing you can say. Don't you get it?" Teresa hissed. "Nothing can take back what you've done. Nothing will ever bring Damien back." She eyed the reptile sack at her feet. "All that's left for me to do now is mete out justice."

"What ... what are you talking about?" Lindsay stammered.

"Brom and Beretta are very special to me," Teresa answered, softening her tone. "They're the only native snakes I own. I caught them myself a few years back."

Lindsay took a heaving breath. Her eyes flicked around in desperation as if realizing what was coming and searching for some last-minute way out of her impossible predicament. "You ... you own other snakes too?"

Teresa grinned at her. "I have three more babies at home. Empress, my pit viper, a krait called Achilles, and my black mamba, Medusa. She's the newest member of our family, and the feistiest."

Lindsay wet her lips, her breathing growing ever more audible in the night air. "Aren't venomous snakes illegal to own?"

Teresa shrugged. "Almost anything's available for purchase over the internet if you know how to look for it." She leaned down and loosened the drawstring on the reptile bag. "I know you're desperate to keep me talking but it's time to wrap things up here."

Lindsay yelped, wriggling another inch or two into the brush. "I'm begging you, Teresa. I know you're upset and hurt, but you're not thinking straight."

"Trust me, I've thought this through very carefully," Teresa replied. "You stuck a knife in my heart twice, so that's what you're going to get in return. Brom is for stealing my father, and Beretta is for killing Damien."

"I didn't kill your brother!" Lindsay howled. "You have to believe me! Please, it wasn't me!"

"*Not I,* said the pig, the cat, and the rat," Teresa mocked in a sing-song tone, reaching for her reptile grabber. "Do you know that story—The Little Red Hen? My father used to read that to me when I was a kid. He said he wanted me to learn from her work ethic." She laughed. "You know what struck me the most? In the end, she did what had to be done all by herself."

"It was Heather! My friend, Heather Nelson," Lindsay blurted out.

Teresa stiffened, and then turned slowly to look at her with narrowed eyes. "What are you talking about?"

"The night Damien died. Heather was following him. She wanted to find out where he lived. He ... he raped her younger sister at a party."

"You're lying," Teresa growled.

"It's the truth," Lindsay protested. "Heather wanted to confront him that night. She brought a gun in the car with her. He was fleeing from her when he crashed. He was injured but still alive. He begged her to help him but she ... she left him there to die. I wanted her to call 911, but she wouldn't. I tried to save your brother!"

For a long moment, Teresa stared coldly at her. Fishing

the rag out of her pocket, she stuffed it back into Lindsay's mouth. Wordlessly, she reached her reptile grabber into the sack and lifted out Brom. "This is for Bill. I hope he was worth it," she said, as she swung the snake in Lindsay's direction and released it. Lindsay screamed, raising her bound arms in a futile defense. Brom struck, burying his fangs into her thumb before slithering off into the night. Lindsay rolled over, attempting to crawl on her belly toward the trail. Teresa grabbed the end of her athletic shirt and flipped her over. "You're not going anywhere. We're not done here yet." She reached for the reptile grabber again and carefully extracted an irate Beretta. "This is for Damien," she said, brandishing the enraged snake.

Writhing in a desperate attempt to get out of striking range, Lindsay succeeded in spitting out the rag. "Your brother was a scumbag!" she screamed. "He deserved what he got!"

Teresa dropped the snake on her chest and observed with satisfaction as Beretta sank her fangs into Lindsay's cheek. She watched her baby glide off through the brush and then sat back down on the tree stump to wait for the venom to take effect.

34

Back at her house, Teresa sank down on the sagging couch surrounded by her dogs and pulled out Lindsay's phone. She had checked it earlier, thrilled to discover it was unlocked—presumably as Lindsay had been running a fitness app tracking her mileage, heartbeat, and a host of other statistics as she biked. It was a stroke of good fortune that would hopefully make Teresa's job of finding Heather Nelson that much easier. If she was a friend of Lindsay's, then her contact information had to be in here.

Teresa had found the phone in a pocket in Lindsay's biker shorts after she'd checked to make sure she was no longer breathing. Once she'd untied her wrists and ankles, she dragged her body through the brush to the edge of the trail and tossed her mangled bike a few feet away. For the final touch, she had placed the rock she used to incapacitate her beneath her head and stepped back to admire her handiwork. It looked every bit the horrific accident it was meant to mimic, and she had driven away afterward satisfied Brom and Beretta had earned their freedom.

Scrolling through Lindsay's contacts, she soon landed on the name: *Heather Nelson*. She studied the information dispassionately. Now that Lindsay had been taken care of, she would concentrate all her efforts on finding the monster who had mercilessly left her brother to die. She gritted her teeth in frustration when she saw that Heather Nelson's current home address was in LA. Teresa had never been a city person. The thought of having to navigate around the inner workings of an urban metropolis seething with people and frenetic activity gave her major anxiety. Not to mention the fact that a trip to LA would mean leaving her babies behind once again. But the biggest hurdle of all would be taking care of business in a city with a host of potential witnesses. Teresa was more at ease in remote locations where the only cameras recording activity on the ground were the sharp eyes of the hawks circling overhead.

Glancing at the note section in Heather Nelson's contact details, Teresa saw Lindsay had entered a birthdate along with the words, *Integrity Investigations*. Curious, she pulled out her laptop and Googled the company. A website popped up, and right there on the home page was a headshot of Heather Nelson, along with several glowing testimonials from satisfied clients. Teresa grunted in anger and tossed the phone onto the pile of trash and magazines that littered the coffee table.

Things had just become complicated. She was dealing with a private investigator—one of the best in the business, if the raving accounts from her clients were to be believed. Gaining access to her world would not be as simple as it had been with the all-too-trusting Lindsay Robinson. Up against a professional PI, Teresa would be at a serious disadvantage, especially if she were forced to venture on to Heather Nelson's home turf of Los Angeles.

As if sensing her aggravation, one of her dogs perked up his ears and licked her hand.

"Mama's okay, Jax," she soothed. "Lay back down."

Forcing herself to regroup, she dug Lindsay's phone back out of the empty pizza box it had fallen into and studied Heather Nelson's contact details. She wasn't invincible—no one was. There had to be a way Teresa could get to her. She would travel to LA if she had to and take all the time she needed to acclimate herself to Heather Nelson's world. Now that she knew the truth, she couldn't let the monster escape justice. What Heather had done eclipsed even the magnitude of Lindsay's betrayal with her father. She had caused Damien to wreck and then fled the scene, leaving him to die.

Teresa squeezed her fingers into a fist. Her brother had been alive after the crash, but he hadn't been found until early the next morning. Heather Nelson had had the power to save him. She could have placed an anonymous call and alerted the paramedics. But she'd chosen not to. She might as well have switched off his life support—what she'd done was equally egregious.

Teresa picked at the stuffing spilling out from the seat cushion beneath her. And then there was the ugly lie Heather had told Lindsay about Damien raping her sister at a party—more likely he'd rejected her awkward advances. If there had been any truth to it, someone would have come knocking on their door that night. Teresa scowled at Heather's contact photo on the phone. How dare she malign her brother's memory with her lies!

Exiting out of Lindsay's contacts, Teresa perused her emails next. It didn't take long before she discovered a lengthy back-and-forth thread about an upcoming twentieth high school reunion. Her lips curved into a satisfied smile when she spotted Heather Nelson's name in the thread. She checked the other four names: Josh Halverson, Sydney McClintock, Reagan Evans, and Marco Romano—satisfied to see that they were all listed in Lindsay's contacts. Apparently, the six of them had worked on the student council together in their senior year.

As Teresa began reading their banter about high school memories, and their happy, successful lives, rage welled up inside her. They must have known all about Lindsay's affair, but what had they done to stop her? Nothing! They'd likely been covering up for Heather all these years too. She ground her teeth in anger. She would punish them all. Every last one of them. They didn't deserve the lives they had. As for Heather Nelson, posing as a crusader for justice all these years was a clever ploy for a murderer trying to appease her conscience. But Teresa would expose her for what she was when the time was right.

Invigorated, she got to work extracting all the info she needed from Lindsay's contacts and sharing it to her phone. Next, she combed through the emails and texts between the group and forwarded herself copies of everything pertinent to the reunion. When she was done, she sank back on the couch, absentmindedly rubbing Jax's ears, a plan slowly coming together in her mind.

She would begin with a surprise introduction at the high school reunion, a hint of what was to come—something to let them know that the crimes they had committed had not been forgotten. A floral arrangement would be in order: forget-me-nots. Symbolic, yet subtle. After that, she would begin to mess with their minds until they each suspected and distrusted the other. In the end, they would turn on Heather like a pack of rabid dogs.

She would destroy their property, their livelihoods, their relationships—whatever it took to satisfy the burning thirst inside for revenge. Ultimately, she would eliminate the monster herself.

"Game on, PI Nelson!" Teresa muttered under her breath. "Let's see how the hunter fares when she's being hunted."

35

Heather turned onto the dirt lane that led up to the remote farmhouse where Teresa lived. Her eyes swept the yard cluttered with old tires, broken pots, random piles of lumber, trash bags, and miscellaneous rusted appliances. There was no sign of Josh's jeep, but that didn't mean to say it wasn't hidden in the barn that sat a hundred or so feet from the house. A frenzied barking greeted her as soon as she turned off her car. She sat quietly for several minutes, waiting to see if a pack of dogs would descend on her, all the while watching the house for any sign of Teresa—the faintest shadow at a window, or the twitch of a curtain, revealing her presence. Unzipping her backpack, she pulled out her utility knife and pocketed it before double checking her concealed weapon. She was under no illusions that she was going to be able to talk her way out of this situation. Teresa had already proven that she was extremely dangerous and unpredictable.

After exiting her car, Heather cautiously approached the front door, keeping a careful eye out for anyone hiding in the trees surrounding the property. To her surprise, the door was ajar. Gingerly, she pushed it fully open, wincing as the splintered wood scraped over the cracked tile floor. It looked like the dogs had made a chew toy out of the door. "Teresa!" she called out. "Are you here? We need to talk."

Other than the nonstop barking coming from the back of the house, there was no response. As the dogs hadn't launched themselves at her the minute she'd left the safety of her car, she figured they must be in a locked pen or fenced yard. Taking a quick, steadying breath, she stepped inside and began creeping along the hallway on high alert for a surprise attack. The house stank like a kennel that hadn't been aired out in years. The kitchen was straight ahead, and to Heather's right was another short hallway, piled high with boxes and random household items. She deliberated for only a second or two before turning and heading in that direction. Josh was most likely being kept in one of the bedrooms.

She approached the first room and tried the handle. Inching the door open, she scanned the contents of the space: a jumble of dog pens, dirty blankets and ratty chew toys. Dog hair was matted everywhere, a thick layer embedded in the shabby carpet. Wrinkling her nose, Heather backed away and proceeded to the next door. Turning the handle, she found herself peering in at a filthy bathroom. She was about to pull the door closed again when she noticed a vial and a syringe lying on the sink. Heart racing, she stepped inside and read the label: *acepro-mazine*. After typing it into her phone, she glanced through the results that popped up. It was some type of sedative for animals—dangerous for humans. A chill traveled down her spine. If Teresa had used this on Josh, he was in dire need of medical attention—if it wasn't already too late. Grimacing, Heather took a quick photo of the vial and hurriedly retreated from the room. There was no time to waste.

Pulse racing, she crept toward the last door at the end of the corridor. One hand on the gun concealed beneath her jacket, she twisted the door handle and nudged it open. Her eyes darted around a messy bedroom. The floor was littered with mounds of discarded clothing, and it smelled almost as bad as the room with the dogs' beds. There was no sign of Josh, and no evidence that he'd been here. Heather closed the door and retraced her steps, picking her way through the mess back down the hallway toward the kitchen.

Panic was rapidly welling up inside her. What if this was all a ruse and Josh wasn't here at all? What if he was being held at a different location? She had wasted precious time driving thirty miles out of town to Teresa's remote farmhouse. Maybe this was what she had wanted all along—to mock her PI skills while she killed Josh at another location. But then why had she left the door open? Heather peered tentatively into the kitchen and looked around the deserted space, catching a glimpse of fur through the window. The dogs still hadn't let up barking. Teresa might be lurking outside somewhere.

Heather's gaze fell on another door at the far end of the kitchen. A pantry, perhaps? It seemed odd that there was a key in the lock—maybe to prevent the dogs from getting into the food. Keeping a careful watch over her shoulder, Heather stole across the room and carefully opened the door. The skin on the back of her neck tingled as she took in the unfinished wooden stairs leading down to a gloomy basement. Could this be where Teresa was keeping Josh? The thought had no sooner struck her before a muffled cry for help wafted up the stairs.

"Josh! Is that you?" she called back into the darkness.

The cry came again, louder this time, accompanied by scuffling sounds, as though someone was trying to kick something to get her attention. Adrenalin shot through her. Stopping only long enough to snatch the key from the door, she darted down the steps, her eyes adjusting to the dimly lit space. A tiny rectangular window at the far end of the basement was the only source of natural light. Directly below it sat Josh, bound to a chair, hands tied behind his back. Heather ran to him and yanked the gag from his mouth. She pulled out her knife and set about cutting him free. Released from his bonds, he mumbled something as he fell forward into her arms.

"Josh! What did she do to you?"

He moaned. "A shot. It's hard to breathe."

"Okay, take it easy," Heather soothed. "I'm going to get you out of here."

"She sent me a picture of you tied up," Josh rasped.

"She faked it," Heather said. "It wasn't me."

Josh panted a few breaths. "Why ... is she doing this?"

"I'll explain everything later. There's no time right now. I've got to get you to a hospital. Can you walk to the steps?"

He threw a dubious glance across the room. "I'll try."

Heather quietly assessed their route to freedom. The stairs were only twenty feet from them, but she wasn't strong enough to carry Josh. He would have to muster his strength and walk with whatever support she could lend him. Gripping him under one arm, she helped him up out of the chair. It was only then that she noticed the glass enclosures lining one entire wall. "What is this place?"

Josh took a ragged breath. "She keeps reptiles down here. She's crazy."

Heather peered at the enclosures with revulsion. She

could just about make out a coiled shape in the enclosure closest to them. *Snakes!*

Bile surged up her throat as a disturbing thought struck her. Had Teresa somehow orchestrated the fatal rattlesnake bites that killed Lindsay? A shiver rippled across her shoulders. If that was the case, Damien's twin was even more sick and twisted than she had imagined. "Let's get out of here before she comes back," she urged Josh.

They had taken only a couple of faltering steps before a low-pitched voice washed over them. "I see you made it here in time for the party."

Heather tensed, her eyes widening at the sight of the large-boned woman standing at the top of the basement steps. A long, heavy, brown braid hung limply over one shoulder. It was the woman Aidy had found a picture of on Roy's phone.

"It's over, Teresa," Heather said, her calm tone belying the tension swirling in her gut. "You need to step aside. I have to get Josh to the hospital."

Teresa bared her teeth in a cold smile. "That's heroic, but I'm afraid I can't let you do that. I've already planned the ending to our little soirée, and it doesn't go quite the way you'd like it to. This ends with your death—we both know that—but when I found out about your little crush on Josh, I thought it would be a more interesting twist if you died together."

"You know you don't mean that," Heather responded. "You're angry and hurt, and it's understandable that you want to lash out at someone, but if you kill us, you're only going to end up spending the rest of your life in prison."

"What makes you think I haven't spent my entire life in a prison of your making?" Teresa snapped as she descended a step. "You murdered Damien and now you're going to pay.

You think you're a hot shot PI, but it turns out you're not as clever as your website claims. What you tried to cover up has come back to bite you after all these years."

"I didn't kill your brother," Heather replied. "He made the choice to drink and drive. I followed him because I had to try and make him understand exactly what he'd done to my sister—how it had broken her."

"You can't talk your way out of this," Teresa snarled. "You took a shotgun with you that night. You had every intention of killing Damien. You just got lucky he crashed, otherwise you'd still be locked up right now. Instead, you got to walk away and wash your hands of your crime. You left my brother to die." She paused, narrowing her eyes. "All your friends are suffering now as a consequence of your actions, and you're going to die next—just like Lindsay did, and just like Roy did."

"Roy? I don't understand. What did he have to do with anything?" Heather asked, trying to buy some time to think as she struggled to support Josh's weight.

Teresa gave an indifferent shrug. "He meddled in things he shouldn't have meddled in. He caught me hiding out at his house while I was waiting for you to show up. Of course he went ballistic like the hothead he is. He thought I was working for some guy he owed money to. He took a photograph of me and said he was going to the police with it—he wanted to press trespassing charges. I couldn't let him draw that kind of attention to me." She smirked as she came down another step. "Besides, I needed a scapegoat for the arson."

"How did you know I was going to be at Roy's house?" Heather asked.

Teresa let out a scoffing laugh. "You're the PI. Figure it out!"

"So you were behind it all—the flower delivery, the threats, the arson, the poisoning, even Roy's murder?"

"I wouldn't say everything," a familiar voice said.

Shock ricocheted through Heather's veins when she saw who stepped into view at the top of the stairs.

36

"**R**eagan! What ... what are you doing here?" Heather choked out.

"Help us!" Josh mumbled, stretching a hand in her direction.

Reagan leaned against the door frame, arms folded in front of her, a callous smile playing on her lips. "Oh I'm here to help all right—just not you, Josh."

"What are you talking about?" Heather cried. "Are you ... were you in on this—luring Josh here, drugging him?"

Reagan let out an exasperated sigh. "You and your nauseating schoolgirl crush. You're missing the point as usual. That's the thing about you, Heather. You think you can sail through life without any consequences while the rest of us pay dearly for the mistakes we make."

Heather shook her head in bewilderment. "I don't understand what you mean. Look, whatever happened between us our senior year, you got what you wanted in the end. I don't hold a grudge against you."

Reagan let out a scoffing laugh. "Do you really think that's what this is about? I couldn't care less about squashing your lame campaign for class president." She straightened up and scowled down at Heather. "This is about something much bigger. You didn't just destroy Teresa's life when you left her brother to die like a dog on the side of the road. You destroyed mine too. All these years and I never suspected a thing—not until I got a call from Teresa a few months back. She found my contact information in Lindsay's phone. Once she realized who I was, she told me everything. She said Lindsay made a confession in her dying moments—that you were the reason Damien wrecked his truck and died that night."

Reagan's features twisted and she teetered on the step as if reeling from the impact of her own words. "Damien Kinney was my boyfriend. I couldn't tell anyone I was dating him in high school because my parents didn't like him, or the fact that he was two years older than me. We kept our relationship secret from everyone, other than Teresa, but we had plans to move in together as soon as I graduated. You took all that away from us. After Damien died, I was a lost soul. I ended up with that lowlife Roy—wasted ten years of my life with him." She curled her lips into a cruel smile. "Although, as Teresa pointed out, he did serve a purpose in the end."

"But ... you have a good life now. You have a family," Heather countered. "Your daughter, and Dave."

"Don't you dare bring up Lucy!" Reagan screamed. "She should have been Damien's child. You screwed up everything. Now I'm stuck trying to milk money out of Marco to support his kid because Dave doesn't earn enough to provide for us properly. It's time you paid for what you stole from me."

"You won't get away with this," Heather said.

Reagan arched an amused brow. "Is that a fact? You

think you're such an amazing investigator, but you fell for every piece of bait I laid out for you. Why do you think I included a tribute to Lindsay in the reunion program? To lure you back to Iowa, of course."

"You knew all this time that Teresa killed Lindsay!" Heather spat out. "You'll pay for this, Reagan!"

"No one knows you're here," Teresa cut in abruptly. "My property backs up to national forest land. Don't think for a minute anyone will ever find your graves."

Teresa descended the remaining steps and reached for a long-handed reptile grabber hanging on the wall. She approached one of the glass enclosures and opened the hinged door on the front before expertly scooping up a yellow and black banded snake.

Heather gripped Josh tighter and took a hasty step backward, a knot forming in her throat as Teresa dangled the snake from the grabber. "Let me introduce you to Achilles," she said. "A banded krait from Bangladesh. Stunning specimen, isn't he?"

"This isn't funny, Teresa. Put the snake back and let's talk about this," Heather urged in a calm tone.

"Beautiful things are sometimes dangerous," Teresa continued in a hypnotic tone, tuning out Heather entirely. "Did you know that krait snakes are actually cannibals? They eat other snakes as a matter of course, but they're not adverse to eating other krait snakes either in a pinch. So you see they're not all that unlike us. We humans eat other humans all the time. Not literally, but with the same net result—we destroy each other."

"It doesn't have to be like that though," Heather countered. "Humans can forgive each other too. We have it inside ourselves to show compassion and grace."

Reagan let out a disdainful snort. "You didn't feel that way twenty years ago."

"I was seventeen-years-old, trying to defend my little sister. I made a terrible mistake. I've had to live with the guilt of my choice that night ever since," Heather said quietly. "But we're adults with some life perspective now. Surely we can forgive and move forward."

Teresa cocked her head to one side. "Do I look that weak to you?"

"It takes strength to forgive," Josh chimed in.

Teresa stared at him, a disturbing gleam in her eyes. "Snakes have more strength than most people realize. A single bite from a krait can result in unrecoverable nerve damage. Do you know what that means for you, Josh?"

He made a choking sound at the back of his throat and shook his head.

"It causes paralysis—that little sedative I gave you pales in comparison to what awaits you. In the end, you won't even be able to move your diaphragm to breathe. You'll slowly asphyxiate."

"Enough of the game warden lecture," Reagan called down to her sharply. "Just do it!"

Teresa flashed a chilling grin at Heather and Josh, and then, in one deft movement, flung the krait snake over the floor in their direction.

Time seemed to stand still, a blur of black and yellow, as Heather's brain kicked into gear, her training lending her the reaction speed she needed to draw her weapon, aim, and fire at the reptile.

"No!" Teresa howled, propelling herself forward the second the gunshot rang out. She fell to her knees by the writhing bloodied snake that lay between them. Leaning protectively over it, she swayed back and forth as if in a trance, mumbling incoherently.

Heather wasted no time helping Josh hobble across the room to the wooden staircase. The minute they reached it, the door at the top slammed shut leaving them with only the slit of light that the filthy ground level window allowed. Heather tossed a quick glance over her shoulder at Teresa, but she was still hunched over her dead snake, lost in her world of all-consuming grief.

When Josh finally made it to the top of the stairs, Heather twisted the handle to open the door, but quickly realized something was blocking it. She put her shoulder to it and shoved repeatedly until it burst open, knocking over a small chest that had been dragged in front of it. She fished the basement key from her pocket and locked the door behind her. "Dial 911," she yelled, thrusting her phone into Josh's hands before darting into the hallway.

"Reagan!" she called out. "Where are you? You're not going to get away with this." She listened for a moment, but the only response was a manic barking. Reagan must have gone outside—hopefully she wasn't going to unleash a pack of rabid dogs on them next. Seconds later, Heather heard the sound of an engine. She dashed out through the front door and took aim at the white Subaru emerging from the barn. Undeterred, Reagan accelerated toward her. Heather took aim and fired, blowing out the left front tire. Reagan altered course and tore off down the driveway, engine screaming. Gritting her teeth, Heather fired again, blowing out another tire. Reagan swerved, over-correcting before careening into the ditch a short distance from the main road.

Heather's shoulders sagged, her adrenalin level dropping several notches. Shaking, she lowered her weapon and sank to her knees, relief flooding her system. It was over. She had kept her wits about her and prevailed. The paramedics would be here soon and would take care of Josh. Marco and Sydney no longer needed to fear for their lives. Violet and her baby were safe from any future threats or intimidation. And, hopefully, Teresa would get the help she should have got twenty years ago. As for Reagan, Heather would be glad if she never had to see her pinched face again.

The welcome sound of sirens filled her ears. Moments later, several emergency vehicles turned off the main road and onto the dirt lane. She watched as Reagan was handcuffed and led over to a squad car. The ambulance and a second squad car continued up the driveway, and Heather hurried to greet the paramedics and direct them inside to Josh.

"I think she gave him acepromazine," Heather said as a paramedic checked his vitals. "It's some kind of sedative for animals."

"Everything's going to be all right now," she assured Josh, squeezing his hand as the paramedics loaded him on to a stretcher trolley and wheeled him out to the waiting ambulance. "I'll see you at the hospital shortly."

"I'm Officer Flaherty," one of the police officers said, introducing himself with a dip of his head. "I take it the perpetrator's still in the basement?"

Heather nodded and led the officers over to the basement door. "She keeps her venomous snakes down here, so be careful," she warned them as she turned the key in the lock. "I shot one, but there are several more in the glass enclosures along the wall."

"All right, we'll take it from here," Officer Flaherty replied, drawing his weapon as he stepped in front of her.

He motioned to his partner, and then slowly opened the door. "Police!" he shouted down the stairs. "Hands in the air. We're coming in."

Heather paced back-and-forth across the kitchen floor as she waited for the officers to reappear at the top of the stairs with a handcuffed Teresa in tow. Moments later, a loud crackling of radios erupted, and the two men beat a hasty retreat back up the stairs and slammed the door. "There's a loose snake down there," Officer Flaherty said, visibly shaken. "We're going to have to wait for animal control to get here."

"What?" Heather exclaimed. "Are you sure it isn't dead—the black and yellow one I shot?"

He shook his head. "It had a gray body. It reared up and hissed."

"What about Teresa?" Heather asked.

"She's sitting in the corner with her back against the wall, leaning up against a freezer," he replied. "She was unresponsive when we called to her."

A cold chill went down Heather's spine. She sank down on a kitchen chair to wait while more officers spilled into the farmhouse and began collecting evidence and taping off the house.

Officer Flaherty pulled out a notepad. "I'm going to take a quick statement from you to add to what Josh relayed to the dispatcher. You're Heather Nelson, is that correct?"

Heather nodded. "Yes."

"How do you know Teresa Kinney?"

"I don't—not directly." Heather let out a heavy sigh and proceeded to give him an abbreviated version of everything that had transpired.

"What will happen to the dogs?" she asked, when she was done with her statement.

"We'll work with animal control on rehousing them."

Heather furrowed her brow. "I feel bad for them. They don't understand what's happening."

Officer Flaherty grunted. "They'll be better off out of this flea-ridden hovel. They weren't being properly cared for."

They were interrupted by the arrival of the animal control officers. One of them introduced himself with a grave nod. "Jim Richards, Scott County Animal Control. Any idea what type of snakes we're dealing with?"

"I don't know for sure," Heather answered. "She called the one I shot a banded krait. All I can tell you is that they're venomous."

Jim exchanged a wary glance with his partner.

"I'll accompany you," Officer Flaherty said, reaching for his weapon as he opened the door to the basement. "The perpetrator's still down there."

Heather reached inside her jacket and pulled out her phone to bring Marco and Sydney up to speed on everything that had transpired.

To her relief, the animal control officers emerged from the basement a short time later clutching a reptile sack.

Officer Flaherty followed a few steps behind them, his face grim.

"She's all yours," he said to the waiting paramedics as they reached for their medical bags.

"Is she ... going to make it?" Heather asked, her eyes zigzagging between Officer Flaherty and the animal control officers.

"It doesn't look good," Jim said, a deep cleft forming in his brow. "We don't have anti-venom for exotic snakes around here. A game warden would have known that. This was suicide."

Heather and Josh slowed to a stop and dismounted from their bikes as they neared the memorial tree and plaque that had been erected in Lindsay's honor to replace the makeshift shrine of stuffed animals, cycling jerseys, handwritten notes, and withered flowers that had sprung up in the weeks after her death.

"It's hard to believe she's been gone a year already," Heather said.

Josh rubbed a hand over his jaw. "Yeah, it's still hard to take it in. We had a narrow escape ourselves."

"I can't believe I never made the connection between Bill and Damien. Some investigator I was," Heather said with a sigh.

"How were you supposed to know? You never even saw a picture of Bill when Lindsay was dating him."

Heather tucked her hair behind her ears and knelt down to trace her fingers over the inscription on Lindsay's plaque. "I know. I just wish I'd pushed Lindsay harder at the time to break it off."

"Don't go there. We've talked about this," Josh said.

"Today isn't about the past and regrets; it's about the future and the promises it holds. You know Lindsay would want you to move on and leave your guilt behind once and for all. You're not responsible for other people's actions. Just like Bill wasn't responsible for what Teresa did, no matter how much she tried to blame her father for her miserable life. We all choose our reactions to our circumstances."

A shudder crossed Heather's shoulders. "I still think it's weird how Teresa went to work every day for years, and not a single soul knew she was living with those dangerous reptiles, as well as an entire pack of dogs."

"Don't forget the feral cats," Josh said. "Animal control found six—or maybe it was seven—fully grown cats and several litters of kittens in the barn."

Heather shook her head. "That's nuts. I mean, I get that she had a connection with animals, and she wanted to share her life with them. I love coming home to my little Phoebe. But it seemed more like a strange obsession with her."

"Trauma in a person's life can sometimes lead to animal hoarding," Josh said. "It was pretty evident Teresa resented the fact that her father abandoned her. She felt unloved and powerless watching her family dissolve. She likely projected those emotions and feelings onto her animals. It's sad. At the end of the day she was desperately lonely."

"You have a good heart, Josh Halverson," Heather replied. "Maybe it's the compassionate health professional in you. As the skeptical Los Angeles PI, I tend to read her a little differently. I think there was an evil streak in her that craved power over something lethal. I think she enjoyed the danger of keeping venomous snakes in her home. Just like she enjoyed setting the fire in Marco's restaurant and killing Roy. You heard her—she was devoid of all emotion when she talked about it."

"What shocks me the most is that Reagan was involved. I can't believe she manipulated Teresa into murdering a stranger," Josh mused. "Teresa had no personal beef with Roy. Or Sydney either."

"I can totally see Reagan manipulating Teresa into doing her bidding," Heather said drily. "She hoodwinked me—lured me out here with the whole reunion tribute to Lindsay. Invented that incident on the freeway to make us think she was being targeted. She even told me Dave was going to hire a PI if I didn't investigate the threats. I found out later he never said any such thing. She's always been controlling and good at coercing people into doing what she wants. She pretty much always got her way in high school, or have you forgotten?"

Josh raised his brows. "I remember her twisting our arms only too well. It's her daughter I feel bad for. It's got to be traumatizing knowing your mother's locked up for murder. How do you explain that to the kids on the playground?"

"Thankfully, Lucy still has Dave," Heather said. "He legally adopted her when he and Reagan got married. He's a good guy. Lucy's doing well, all things considered. I check in with them every so often."

"So you do have a heart, after all," Josh said with a wink. "Speaking of kids, how's your niece doing?"

"Vera? She's the most adorable baby you've ever set eyes on," Heather said, unable to stop a grin spreading across her face. Even the thought of her niece was enough to make all her troubles pale into insignificance. Spending time with her was the highlight of her recent trips back to Iowa. "The best part about it is that I think she actually likes me. She smiles when I pick her up. I've never evoked that kind of reaction in a kid before."

"Why *wouldn't* she like you?" Josh said, a grin playing on his face as he pulled her close and kissed her softly on the lips. "I like you. In fact, I like you enough to move my practice all the way out to the West Coast if that's what it takes to be with you."

Heather gave an adamant shake of her head. "No. You would hate it out there. You're too genuine for a place like LA. Believe me, it's a synthetic world, in every sense of the word. Besides, it won't be necessary. I'm coming home."

Josh's eyes widened. He held her at arm's length, studying her expression. "Are you serious?"

"Yes. I've already listed my condo. It should fetch enough to open a PI firm here and buy a comfortable home. I won't be able to earn anything close to the kind of money I'm making in LA, but I have a feeling I'll be enriching my life on a whole deeper level."

Josh wrapped her in his arms and squeezed her tightly. "You've no idea how happy it makes me to hear that."

"And I might never if you don't let me breathe," Heather said with a laugh.

"What made you come to this decision?" Josh asked, releasing her.

Heather shrugged, her gaze landing on Lindsay's plaque. "I've been thinking about what you said the last time I came out here—that people who wander the halls of the past only ever exist. Living is all about stepping into the future and taking risks."

Josh gave her a sheepish grin. "I have to confess I don't remember saying it quite that elegantly. But it sounds good. And I'm glad I said it if it convinced you to take a risk on me."

"The funny thing is, I'm not afraid of taking physical risks," Heather mused. "I do it every day in my job. But I've shied away from taking a risk with my emotions, until now."

"That sounds like a proposal." Josh grabbed her hand and pressed it to his lips, before dropping to one knee. "Trust me, I'm a low risk investment with a guaranteed return. If you'll settle for a lowly psychiatrist who makes good coffee, I'm yours."

Heather laughed and pulled him to his feet. "Let's see if my condo sells first."

Josh clutched his chest in an expression of heartbreak. "I'll keep trying." He picked up his bike and adjusted the baseball cap on his head. "Ready to get out of here?"

"Almost," Heather replied. "Let's go down by the river. There's one last thing I need to do."

They sat on the banks of the Mississippi, heads huddled together, watching the sun go down—a glimmer of sunlight lingering over the swathe of inky water. Heather reached for her backpack and pulled out the hook she had found in the brush near to where Lindsay was murdered.

Josh threw her a tender glance. "Are you sure you're ready to do this now?"

She nodded, squeezing back the stinging tears that threatened.

"Remember what I told you," Josh prompted. "When you let it go, everything goes with it, the guilt, the regret, the walls—everything that's keeping you stuck."

Heather swallowed the knot in her throat as she got to her feet. She inhaled a deep breath and pulled back her right arm. "This one's for you, Lindsay," she choked out. "Free at last!" With a determined grunt, she flung the hook as far as she could out over the rippling darkness. It made a plopping sound, instantly swallowed into the murky depths.

Heather smiled through the tears silently streaking

down her face. The crippling burden of guilt she had been staggering through life with had sunk with the hook to the bottom of the Mississippi River. Her days of dwelling in the past were over. It was time to start dreaming again.

She was at peace at last.

~

NEVER TELL THEM

Ready for another thrilling read with shocking twists and a mind-blowing murder plot? Check out my psychological thriller *Never Tell Them* on Amazon! Releasing May 2021.

How well do you know the stranger next door?
When mysterious, single dad Ray Jenkins moves in to the neighborhood, Sonia is suspicious from the outset that something is amiss. Ray's young son, Henry—traumatized

from the recent loss of his mother—acts like he barely knows his father.

But things soon take a turn for the worse when Ray is involved in a multi-vehicle wreck, and suffers a brain injury and subsequent memory loss. Sonia steps in to care for Henry, but soon becomes alarmed at the disturbing things he tells her. Determined to get to the bottom of who her neighbor really is, she snoops around in his house. The shocking clues she uncovers shake her to the core. Her own life is in danger from the deadly lie he is living.

The more she digs, the more she finds that some lies are best left buried.

- A gripping tale of explosive secrets with a jaw-dropping twist!
-

∽

Do you enjoy reading across genres? I also write young adult science fiction and fantasy thrillers. You can find out more about those titles at **www.normahinkens.com**.

A QUICK FAVOR

Dear Reader,

I hope you enjoyed reading *The Class Reunion* as much as I enjoyed writing it. Thank you for taking the time to check out my books and I would appreciate it from the bottom of my heart if you would leave a review, long or short, on Amazon as it makes a HUGE difference in helping new readers find the series. Thank you!

To be the first to hear about my upcoming book releases, sales, and fun giveaways, sign up for my newsletter at **www.normahinkens.com** and follow me on Twitter, Instagram and Facebook. Feel free to email me at norma@normahinkens.com with any feedback or comments. I LOVE hearing from readers. YOU are the reason I keep going through the tough times.

All my best,
Norma

BIOGRAPHY

NYT and USA Today bestselling author Norma Hinkens writes twisty psychological suspense thrillers, as well as fast-paced science fiction and fantasy about spunky heroines and epic adventures in dangerous worlds. She's also a travel junkie, legend lover, and idea wrangler, in no particular order. She grew up in Ireland, land of make-believe and the original little green man.

Find out more about her books on her website.
www.normahinkens.com

Follow her on Facebook for funnies, giveaways, cool stuff & more!

ALSO BY N. L. HINKENS

Head to my website to find out more about my other psychological suspense thrillers.

www.normahinkens.com/books

- The Silent Surrogate
- I Know What You Did
- The Lies She Told
- Her Last Steps
- The Other Woman
- You Will Never Leave
- The Cabin Below
- The Class Reunion
- Never Tell Them

BOOKS BY NORMA HINKENS

I also write young adult science fiction and fantasy thrillers under Norma Hinkens.

www.normahinkens.com/books

THE UNDERGROUNDERS SERIES - POST-APOCALYPTIC
Immurement
Embattlement
Judgement

THE EXPULSION PROJECT - SCIENCE FICTION
Girl of Fire
Girl of Stone
Girl of Blood

THE KEEPERS CHRONICLES - EPIC FANTASY
Opal of Light
Onyx of Darkness
Opus of Doom

Follow Norma:

Sign up for her newsletter:
https://books.normahinkens.com/VIPReaderClub
Website:
https://normahinkens.com/
Facebook:
https://www.facebook.com/NormaHinkensAuthor/
Twitter
https://twitter.com/NormaHinkens
Instagram
https://www.instagram.com/normahinkensauthor/
Pinterest:
https://www.pinterest.com/normahinkens/

Made in the USA
Coppell, TX
19 March 2022